BANJO

BANJO

GRAHAM SALISBURY

WENDY
LAMB
BOOKS

Text copyright © 2019 by Graham Salisbury
Jacket art copyright © 2019 by Oriol Vidal

All rights reserved. Published in the United States by Wendy Lamb Books, an imprint of Random House Children's Books, a division of Penguin Random House LLC, New York.

Wendy Lamb Books and the colophon are trademarks of Penguin Random House LLC.

Visit us on the Web! rhcbooks.com

Educators and librarians, for a variety of teaching tools, visit us at RHTeachersLibrarians.com

Library of Congress Cataloging-in-Publication Data
Names: Salisbury, Graham, author.
Title: Banjo / Graham Salisbury.
Description: First edition. | New York : Wendy Lamb Books,
an imprint of Random House Children's Books, [2019] |
Summary: Danny, a rising rodeo star whose border collie, Banjo,
has been wounded by neighbors, and Meg, who has a way with animals,
come together to keep Banjo safe, aided by Danny's brother. |
Identifiers: LCCN 2018038802 (print) | LCCN 2018044435 (ebook) |
ISBN 978-0-307-97561-4 (ebook) | ISBN 978-0-375-84264-1 (trade) |
ISBN 978-0-375-94069-9 (lib. bdg.) | ISBN 978-0-375-84265-8 (pbk.)
Subjects: | CYAC: Human-animal relationships—Fiction. | Border collie—
Fiction. | Dogs—Fiction. | Ranch life—Oregon—Fiction. | Rodeo—Fiction. |
Horses—Training—Fiction. | Oregon—Fiction.
Classification: LCC PZ7.S15225 (ebook) |
LCC PZ7.S15225 Ban 2019 (print) | DDC [Fic]—dc23

The text of this book is set in 12-point Sabon MT Pro.
Interior design by Jaclyn Whalen

Printed in the United States of America
10 9 8 7 6 5 4 3 2 1
First Edition

For Copper
The best dog I have ever known

And other dogs I have loved:
Nicky
Chloe
Trixie
Rocky
Roo

And the ones I have tolerated:
Sergeant
Boomer

1

Danny Mack was pretty sure he'd just lost his thumb.

He'd caught the steer but lost control of his rope. He tried to wrap it around the saddle horn but wasn't quick enough. When his horse, Pete, dug in and pulled back, the rope snapped into place and ripped his roping glove clean off his hand.

"Ow!"

Danny grimaced and gaped at it. No blood. And his thumb was still there. He shook out the sting.

His best friend, Ricky, ran over from where he'd been manning the roping chute. "You all right?"

"I think so."

Summer vacation had just begun, and Danny and his dad were in their home arena practicing team roping, getting ready to compete in the Jefferson County Fair and Rodeo in a couple of weeks. Ricky and Danny's brother Tyrell were helping out. Tyrell was seventeen, four years older than Danny. As a team, Danny and his dad competed in community and open rodeos. Danny was the header, roping the horns. Dad, the heeler, roping the back feet. They were good at it, because they practiced.

Dad, who'd caught the steer's two back legs, loosened his rope and loped over on Mandingo. "You hurt?"

"Stings," Danny said, squeezing his hand. He had to focus on his dally—his wrap around the saddle horn.

Dad leaned in for a closer look. "You'll live. But be more focused. Roping's dangerous, which is why we're out here getting it right."

"Yes, sir."

Tyrell drew up on his horse, Half-Asleep. "What happened?"

"Rope almost took my thumb off."

"Looks like it's still there."

"Yep."

Danny turned in his saddle. His glove was lying in the dirt by the fence. He whistled. "Banjo! Get my glove."

Banjo, his border collie, snapped up, got it, and ran it over.

Danny leaned down and took it. "Good boy."

He pulled the glove back on.

Tyrell rode off to free the steer from the ropes and herd it back to Ricky at the chute.

"Let's give it one more run and call it a day," Dad said.

Danny nodded and coiled his rope. He loped Pete around the practice pen to calm himself down. *This time, focus!*

Tyrell and Ricky got the steer back into the chute.

Banjo trotted back to his place by the fence.

Danny backed Pete into the box on the left side of the chute, where he'd wait until the steer was released. Dad backed Mandingo in on the right.

When the steer was in place, Ricky glanced at Danny. "Ready when you are."

The idea was to stay in the box as short a time as possible. Get in, get ready, and hope the steer got up to the gate with his head aimed forward. That was the unknown, the steer.

Dad nodded to Danny.

Danny nodded to Ricky.

Ricky slammed the gate open. *"Haw!"*

The steer burst out running.

A split second later, Danny spurred Pete ahead.

The hardest part wasn't the roping but the riding, and Danny's balance astonished anyone who watched him. Dad once told him that he was about as good a rider as it was possible to be.

Danny stayed to the left, with Pete's nose even with the steer's hip.

Dad on Mandingo flew out of the heeler's box, staying about ten feet off to the right, keeping the steer on a straight path so Danny could get a good shot at its head.

Danny threw his loop—a clean catch over both horns. He made his dally around the saddle horn, doing it right this time. He slowed and pulled the steer to the left so the steer's hind legs flayed out as it turned.

Dad threw his loop and caught both back feet. He hadn't missed all day. He made his dally and turned Mandingo to face Danny and Pete, the horses pulling the ropes taut, the caught steer between them.

Dad nodded. "Do it like that two weeks from now and we'll be all right."

"Yep," Danny said. "Just like that."

"Not bad, little brother," Tyrell called. "You too, old man."

Dad grunted.

Ricky and Tyrell removed the head protector from the steer's horns and released the steer into the pasture. Dad and Tyrell took their horses into the barn.

Danny sat his horse, looking down on Ricky. "What you doing after this?"

"Chores, I guess."

"Want to do something later?"

"Like what?"

Danny looked back at the barn and out toward the pasture. "Oh, I don't know. Watch grass grow?"

Ricky grinned and walked over to his bike to head home. Danny rode Pete alongside him, while Banjo sniffed through the weeds.

"Thanks for helping out today," Danny said.

"No problem. You'd do it for me."

"Not with bulls, I wouldn't."

Ricky laughed.

Ricky was a junior bull rider, and Danny was not a fan of bulls. One wild kick and they could kill you. Danny knew of a rodeo bull from Texas that weighed 1,900 pounds. That one could kick you from Oregon to South Carolina. As a junior rider, Ricky rode bulls that were between 500 and 1,000 pounds.

Danny said, "You have more guts than brains."

Ricky laughed. "You're just jealous."

He whistled for Banjo, squatting as he trotted over. "You

take care of that wimp on the horse, you hear? He needs help."

Banjo nosed Ricky's hand.

Ricky looked up. "Guess he sees my point."

"Get outta here," Danny said, smiling. "Wanna do some fishing? If not later today, then next week?"

"Sure. Call me." Ricky gave him a thumbs-up and rode off.

Danny whistled and slapped his thigh. "Banjo! Come!"

Banjo raced over and leaped. Danny caught him by the skin on the back of his neck and lifted him into the saddle. Banjo licked his face.

"I think you've earned yourself a treat, don't you?"

Together, they rode back to the barn.

2

Five days later, Danny bolted up in the middle of the night. He thought he'd heard a shot.

His room was still. The light in the yard cast a rectangular shadow across his wall.

Ca-rack!

Another shot. From a rifle.

Then two more.

The floorboards in the room above him creaked. Tyrell was up. Danny squinted at his clock.

2:49.

He got up and crossed to the window. The yard, the drive, and the trucks were gray under the light near the barn.

Past the barn, the corral was empty. The working pen and pasture beyond lay silent and ghostly, edged by a dark line of trees.

Light from the hall flooded his room. His brother stood in the doorway dragging a T-shirt over his head. "You hear that?"

Tyrell was six foot one, with a scraggly brown beard, bright blue eyes, and a thin scar in his left eyebrow.

"Rifle?" Danny said.

Tyrell nodded. "You coming?"

"Yep."

Danny pulled on sweats and stumbled into his boots as he followed Tyrell out. "Is Dad up?"

"Apparently not."

Danny looked up the stairs. Dad's door was open, but the room was dark. Probably slept right through it. He'd come in around midnight. Dad was an independent trucker and was often gone two, three days at a time.

Tyrell reached into the closet by the front door and grabbed the Winchester 94, their grandfather's hunting rifle.

They jogged around the barn, then out into the pasture and up a ridge, where they looked down onto their neighbor's land and the wide valley that spread east. Pinpricks of light winked in the black far distance.

"Can't see a thing," Danny whispered.

Tyrell aimed the rifle forward, finger outside the trigger guard, ready. "Those shots came from this direction."

Danny squinted down the grassy slope, trying to see. The ridge where they stood was on their property. A fence below separated their place from the Brodies' sheep ranch.

"See anything?"

Tyrell didn't answer.

Danny looked back. "Where's Banjo?"

"Barn, I guess."

Danny was instantly alert. The only reason Banjo wouldn't be with him right now was that something was wrong.

"He'd have heard us and come out," Danny said. "He'd be here."

"True."

"Something's weird."

Tyrell let up on the rifle. "Whatever it is, I sure can't see it."

Danny glanced again into the black silence, then backed away and jogged after Tyrell, heading to the house.

He checked Banjo's bed in the hay shed. Empty. "Banjo. You here, boy?"

"Check the barn," Tyrell said. "I'll look around back."

Danny ran into the barn.

Nothing.

"He ain't out back," Tyrell said from the door. "Find anything?"

Danny shook his head.

Tyrell tucked the rifle into the crook of his arm, muzzle down. The night was so silent it made Danny shiver. "Think we should wake Dad up?"

"Let him sleep. What could he do that we ain't done already?"

"What about Banjo?"

"He'll show up sooner or later . . . 'less he's the one got shot."

"That's not funny."

"Wasn't meant to be."

Tyrell put a hand on Danny's shoulder. "We'll find him. Maybe the shots spooked him."

They headed into the house.

Inside, Danny got his sleeping bag and took it out to the hay shed, where Banjo always slept. *He'll come back. He has to come back.*

He stood alone in the eerie silence, feeling strange and empty without his dog. It felt like when his mom left. Danny was four then. After she left, he saw her every other week for a couple of years, but she eventually married a rancher and moved to California. Danny liked him. But even though his mom called them every week, and flew him and Tyrell down to California twice a year, she was an empty place inside him.

"Banjo!" Danny called.

All he got back was the faint yip of a coyote out on the distant plain. It was the most lonesome sound he'd ever heard.

3

Just hours after the late-night shooting at the Mack place, the sun rose into the blue of a cloudless summer day.

Twenty miles up the road near the old western town of Sisters, Meg Harris and her best friend, Josie, carried a saddle and blanket out into the middle of a covered, open-sided arena. Meg pitched the saddle upright on the ground. Josie set the saddle blanket on top of it, then helped Meg adjust her clip-on wireless microphone.

"Nervous?" Josie asked, her voice low.

"A little."

"You'll be all right."

Meg nodded. "Thanks for coming."

"You think I'd miss a show like this?"

"I hope I don't get a horse I can't handle."

Josie gave Meg a quick hug and headed over to the stands to sit with Meg's family and their other friends from 4-H. Meg was glad they were all there. She didn't want to mess up in front of them. But that was what a 4-H public demonstration was all about—learning by doing. Delivering on your ideas. Still, a horse could be unpredictable, even dangerous, especially if it'd been abused or neglected.

Please, please, please . . . no risky horses.

The view on one side of the arena was of high-country forest below a line of sharp-edged mountains called the Three Sisters. Meg let her gaze rest there as she tried to calm her breathing.

Air in.

Air out.

Long, deep breaths.

Could she really do what she'd promised in her flyer?

```
           4-H demonstration.
Thirteen-year-old girl will put a saddle on
 any horse anyone brings her, broke or not.
      Just don't bring a biter . . .
         she might bite back.
```

She'd put that last part in as a joke.

I can do this, I can do this.

But Meg had a secret—she had yet to put a saddle, or even a halter, on one of her own horses, a half-wild mustang she called Amigo.

She turned back to look at the people in the bleachers.

She smiled, seeing her brothers looking so serious. Even though her mom had to drag them out of bed, Meg didn't care. Jacob, seventeen, and Jeremy, fifteen, were giving her their full attention.

Mom waved, and Meg lifted her chin.

"Learn by doing," Meg whispered. The 4-H slogan. She and Josie had learned most of their life skills at 4-H—head, heart, hands, and health.

She'd tacked flyers up all over town and even put a few

up over in Bend, Redmond, and Prineville, and at the store in Camp Sherman. Sisters was only about ten blocks long, but in the summer it was crammed with tourists and cars and RVs. Maybe that's why so many people were here today—around fifty. She'd expected ten to fifteen.

Meg tapped the small wireless microphone clipped to her shirt.

"Thank you for coming to my demonstration," she said, hands trembling.

Jeez! Get hold of yourself.

"My name is Meg Harris. Today I'm going to show how anyone with a little patience can put a saddle on a difficult horse."

As the crowd waited, her heart thumped; she could actually feel it thundering in her ears.

"So . . . uh . . . did anyone . . . bring a horse? I mean . . . an ornery one?"

People laughed, turning to see if there were any takers.

Meg stood straight, smiling. Her amplified voice made her feel bigger than she was.

"Heck, yeah," a man in a tan hat called. "I'm just not so sure I should turn him loose on you. He's a real doozy. You could sooner saddle a jackrabbit."

Louder laughter.

Now Meg grinned. "Bring him on in."

The man went out to his trailer and returned with a bug-eyed gray horse. The gray tossed its head and pranced when the man led it into the area. Not a big horse, but skittish.

"Are you really thirteen, miss?" the man said. "You look awful young."

"I'll be fourteen in seven months."

He rubbed his chin.

"I can handle him," Meg said, trying not to let the nervous horse make *her* nervous.

The man leaned into her microphone. "If you can get a saddle on this volcano, I'll eat my hat."

He lifted his Stetson as everyone cheered and hooted.

The noise made the gray rear up. He crow hopped sideways, and the man slapped its flank with the end of the lead rope to keep him in line.

He looked at Meg. "You sure you know what you're doing?"

"I wouldn't be in here if I didn't."

He shook his head. "You're one brave girl."

"Call me Meg," she said, and reached for the lead.

The man in the tan hat walked away, leaving Meg with the gray horse. "My daughter rode him for about a month," he said over his shoulder. "Then she went off to college. He ain't been saddled in three years."

He let himself out of the arena and leaned his arms on the rail to watch. "His name's Mr. Gray Hat," he called. "Should've called him Mr. Gray Wolverine."

4

After the shooting, Danny slept in the hay shed, where Banjo usually slept.

At daylight, he opened his eyes and bolted up.

Still no Banjo.

He grabbed his sleeping bag and hurried into the house to check the time. Seven o'clock. He'd overslept by two hours.

He had chores . . . but something was very wrong.

He had to search for Banjo.

Next to his bed sat a wooden chair and a night table with a lamp and a clock inside a silver horseshoe. The top of his dresser was lost under a herd of trophies and ribbons and junior rodeo belt buckle awards. His walls were covered with rodeo posters.

Where are you, Banjo?

He changed into his jeans and pulled on his boots and a white T-shirt.

He quickly brushed his teeth and ran wet fingers through his hair, then looked out the window. Dad was striding toward the barn.

Danny grabbed his hat, ran to the kitchen, took a long

gulp of orange juice from the container in the fridge, and headed out the door.

"Banjo!" he called, running toward the pastures.

Dad poked his head out of the barn. "Whoa, slow down there. What's up?"

"Have you seen Banjo? He's missing."

Dad turned to look back. "That's odd. He should be following me around like always." He frowned. "Tyrell told me what happened last night, before he took off for work."

Danny squinted out toward the trees.

Dad followed his gaze. "Maybe he's sick and holed up somewhere. Dogs do that."

"Yeah . . . maybe."

"Listen, I've got to run a load over to Portland today. Be back sometime tonight."

"All right."

"How's about riding the fence this morning? Make sure everything's as it should be. You might scrub out the water trough in the east pasture, too. Oh, and set out that new salt lick I got, would you?"

"I can do that."

Dad put his hand on Danny's shoulder and squeezed. "Gotta go. See you tonight."

Danny watched his father drive off, then put his hat on and headed into the barn. He set the new salt lick near the water trough, then grabbed a hand-tied halter off its hook in the tack room and went out to the practice pen. There was a shady spot by the fence where Banjo sometimes slept during the day.

He tried whistling.

Nothing.

"Where *are* you?"

In the west pasture, he found the steers and calves grazing. They looked up and stared at him.

Danny whistled. "Banjo! Here, boy!"

He kept walking.

Farther out, he spotted all four horses looking his way.

"Pete," he called.

His horse perked his ears forward.

Danny took the halter and held it up, and Pete, his eleven-year-old gelding, started over, the three other horses trailing close behind.

Danny greeted each one, scratching their foreheads and running a hand down their smooth necks. One mare and three geldings made a peaceful combination.

Danny took a long look in every direction.

No dog.

"Have you guys seen Banjo?"

Pete blinked as Danny slipped the halter over his ears. Danny was proud of the work he'd done with his horse. They trusted each other. "Come on, Pete. We got chores to do and a dog to find."

With the lead loose in his hands, Danny started back toward the barn. Pete bobbed off his right shoulder, following.

In the barn, Danny checked Pete's feet, brushed him, saddled him, and led him outside. He climbed into the saddle and was about to head out to the north pasture when movement caught his eye. He stood in the stirrups to get a better look.

A white pickup was barreling up the drive, trailing an angry cloud of gray dust.

5

Meg clipped a long lead rope to Mr. Gray Hat.

The gray threw his head and danced away, then, at Meg's urging, began circling the arena at a trot.

She let Mr. Gray Hat run on the long lead, allowing him to get comfortable with her and with his new situation.

She stood out in the middle, her eyes pinned on the horse.

In a few minutes, he seemed to become more fluid, almost relaxed. Meg knew then that this was a good horse. But three years of neglect had made him cranky.

She tugged on the lead. Mr. Gray Hat slid to a stop. He lowered his head and eyed her.

She approached slowly, her hand extended so the horse could smell her, like you'd come up on an unknown dog.

Mr. Gray Hat stood his ground. He blew and stretched his neck.

Meg inched closer.

The gray snorted and jerked away.

Meg pulled him back and again reached out.

This time he held, and Meg ran her hand over his nose, which he seemed to like. She stepped closer and gently rubbed his face and neck.

As if under some kind of spell, the horse dropped his head low, then lower still, his eyes half-closed. A lump rose in Meg's throat. *You poor thing. All you needed was for someone to pay attention to you.*

The spectators were silent.

Meg slipped Mr. Gray Hat's worn leather halter off and replaced it with the one in her back pocket. It was bright red and hand-tied. To this she attached the long lead, with two thin strips of cowhide on the end, called a popper.

Meg sent him around the arena in a clean, swift trot. When Mr. Gray Hat started to take off, Meg shook the rope sharply and spun his hindquarters away by tapping his flank with the popper.

The horse whirled around, stopped, and stood still, looking at her with surprise. For a moment his ears flattened back, a sign of anger.

But they didn't stay there.

Meg whispered a few soft words and again held out her hand.

The man in the tan hat shook his head in disbelief as his horse walked toward her and stood, head down, as if shy.

Meg cooed, her voice falling softly from the speakers. "Easy, now. We're doing fine. Yeah."

Again, she sent him around the arena, this time at an easy trot, giving him less and less lead rope so he'd close in around the saddle and blanket standing upright in the middle.

Mr. Gray Hat circled and circled, until his curiosity got

the best of him. He broke stride and moved in toward the saddle and blanket.

"There we go, now," Meg whispered. "There we go."

She waited, watching.

The horse quickly lost interest and looked up to stare at the crowd, as if remembering that they were there. This caused a sprinkle of laughter.

He looked back and stepped closer to the saddle and checked out the smell of it.

"This is where patience comes in," Meg told the spectators in a low voice. "You have to let the horse have a say in the process."

Mr. Gray Hat picked up the saddle blanket in his teeth and shook it.

The crowd roared with delight.

Meg smiled when she saw Josie standing and clapping.

"This horse has a sense of humor," Meg said, taking the blanket back.

"And you, young lady, have a magic touch," the man in the tan hat called out.

The gray looked over at him. More laughter.

"Okay, you little monkey," Meg said. "Now you're showing off."

Meg grinned and looked toward her audience. "You don't make a horse learn something, you *let* him learn it."

She took the saddle blanket and rubbed it about Mr. Gray Hat's shoulders and withers. He seemed almost content with all the attention.

He stood perfectly still as Meg placed the blanket on

his back. She lifted the saddle up against her hip and without taking her eyes off his, or her hand off the lead, lightly swung it into place.

The gray scooted forward a step, and Meg wiggled the lead. He lifted his head but held still.

Then, whispering softly, Meg slipped around to the other side and caught up the cinch with one hand, loosened the latigo strap with the other, and gently drew it up firm about the belly.

When Mr. Gray Hat crow hopped to the side, Meg soothed him until he was still.

The gray was saddled.

The crowd stood and clapped and whistled.

Let's see how far we can take this. Meg put a foot into the stirrup and climbed into the saddle.

Mr. Gray Hat sidestepped, then backed away and reared up on his hind legs. Meg leaned forward so she wouldn't be thrown off the back, grabbing his mane and the saddle horn. "Easy, boy, easy."

Mr. Gray Hat bucked once and broke into a stiff-legged trot. Meg rode him around the arena, and as she did, he settled into a smooth and fluid lope.

After two laps, she reined him in near the stands. The gray pranced with his head high, skittish but responsive to Meg's hand.

She'd done it.

"This isn't magic," she told the crowd. "Anyone can do it if they're willing to take the time. You just have to learn the horse's way of talking to you. Simple horse language.

Nobody, and no horse, likes to be bullied or forced into doing something, right?"

She looked over to the man in the tan hat. "Now, come on out here, mister, and eat your hat."

The audience roared as he hunched out into the arena, the brim of his hat in his teeth.

6

The white truck coming up the drive braked hard between the house and the barn. It was Mr. Brodie, their neighbor.

Danny nudged Pete across the pen to the fence.

Mr. Brodie got out and started for the house, dust from his abrupt stop churning around him.

"Over here," Danny called.

Mr. Brodie turned and strode over in his coveralls and sweat-stained straw hat.

Looking down from atop Pete, Danny was about to say hello, but the pinched look on Mr. Brodie's face stopped him.

Danny hunched forward, his forearms resting on the saddle horn. "I'm sorry, Mr. Brodie, but Dad's not home."

Mr. Brodie's usual way was to spend a minute or two small talking before he got to his business.

But not today. "We got a problem, you and me."

"We do?"

"It's your dog."

Danny froze, then glanced over at the truck and saw the rifle in the window rack. It would only be there if he were going hunting. It wasn't hunting season. A wave of terror ran through him.

Danny dismounted and stood holding the reins, the two of them separated by the fence. "What's the problem?"

"Thought you'd of trained that dog by now, Danny. But he ain't trained at all. Him and a pack of dogs was over to my place in the middle of the night, trying to take down my sheep. My boys heard 'em and ran out and chased 'em off with a rifle. Billy winged one of 'em. Said it might have been that dog of yours."

Danny's legs weakened. He leaned against Pete.

Mr. Brodie glared, his eyes like small brown marbles.

"Banjo doesn't chase sheep, Mr. Brodie."

"I told you when you got him feral dogs can't be trusted, even if they's been domesticated. And now he's gone back to his old ways. I can't have dogs taking down my livestock. He's got to go. Now."

Danny balled his fists to hide his trembling fingers. "Banjo isn't a wild dog." It was all he could think of to say.

"My boys could have shot him dead, but because it was your dog, they didn't. Out of courtesy. Now we got to decide what you're going to do about it."

"How . . . how could they tell it was my dog? It was dark."

Mr. Brodie squinted. Danny thought he might be thinking about saying how flat-out rude he was for a boy his age.

"You'll know when he comes home with a flesh wound. I won't put up with it no longer. I've had three attacks in two years."

"Those were coyotes."

"Dogs ain't no diff'rent. You got to put that wild one of yours down."

Danny's jaw dropped. *I'm not hearing this. This is our neighbor, a friend.* "You can't mean that, Mr. Brodie, I—"

"Oh, I mean ever word."

"Well . . . I . . . no, sir . . . nobody's shooting my dog."

"You sure your daddy ain't here?"

"Yes."

"When's he back?"

Danny stared at Mr. Brodie. *This isn't happening.*

Mr. Brodie glared, then grunted and headed to his truck. "This ain't over."

Danny clenched and released his fists as the truck drove off.

His mind whirled as he headed over toward the barn with Pete.

Mr. Brodie would come back. And Danny knew Dad would have to agree with him. They'd been neighbors for all of Danny's life, and each of them had had trouble with coyotes and wild dogs. When you saw them attacking your livestock, you shot them. And the law had no problem with it.

Danny remembered what Dad had told him and Tyrell seven years ago, when he'd first brought Banjo home. *One thing you boys need to keep in mind is that this dog came from the wild. The guy I got him from thinks he was once domestic, but still, we don't know how he's going to act around the horses. I'm trusting you to keep a close eye on him. If he shows the slightest urge to worry the livestock, I need to know.*

Maybe he was wild once, Danny thought. But Banjo's a good dog, and he's never chased their sheep.

If he shows the slightest urge to worry the livestock, I need to know.

If what Mr. Brodie said was true, he'd have to give Banjo up.

Danny staggered and leaned against Pete.

Find Banjo.

Must find Banjo.

7

Meg Harris's home sat at the back of an open field with towering ponderosa pines on both sides of a long gravel drive. A rust-red barn on the left, a house on the right.

Alone in a pen behind the barn, a five-year-old bay mustang with a black mane lifted its head as Meg and her family drove in after Meg's 4-H demonstration. The horse had white socks on three legs and a ragged, off-center white blaze that shot down his forehead like a drunken lightning bolt.

His name was Amigo.

Meg had had him for three months. He'd been one of hundreds of wild horses caught up in last year's Bureau of Land Management's gather in Wyoming. A man had adopted him, but he and Amigo never took to each other. So he'd put him up for sale.

Meg's parents agreed to let her buy the horse, with her own money, if he looked good. Just the fact that the horse was unwanted made her want him.

Her brother Jacob drove her over.

"You'll never tame that one," the owner said. "He's wild as a wolf."

The mustang was in a small pen. Meg and Jacob stood at

the fence and watched it awhile. It was wild-eyed, scarred, and snorty. Its ribs showed, with nicks all over his legs. The horse tried to climb the enclosure, banging and kicking the rails.

Jacob winced. "I don't know, sis. That horse might not let you or anyone else get near it."

"He's not used to being penned up."

Jacob looked at the owner. "You ride it yet?"

"*Ride* it? I can barely put a rope around its neck. I thought I could break him, but I don't want to get killed trying."

"I'll take him," Meg said, pulling out a wad of cash. "This enough?"

The guy grabbed the money and stuffed it into his pocket without counting it. "More than enough."

Now, Meg called over to Amigo as she got out of the Jeep. "Hello, my sweet. Did you miss me today?"

Her dad laughed. "*Sweet?*"

"You'll see."

"Looking forward to it."

Meg had another horse, a ten-year-old mare named Molly Montana. Didn't flick an ear when you put a saddle on her.

This was the day Meg would risk introducing Molly to Amigo. You never really knew, but she believed the two horses would get along.

An hour later, Meg brushed Molly's sleek, silky black coat in the cool interior of the barn. "Amigo's going to think he's died and gone to heaven when you walk into that pasture to meet him."

Meg hugged Molly's neck, hoping that was true.

So far the day had gone well. At the demonstration, a woman had jokingly told her that from here on out, she'd be known around town as the Ornery-Horse Whisperer of Sisters. Meg smiled, though she believed that *ornery* just meant uncared-for or misunderstood.

"How 'bout it, Molly-girl?" she said. "You want to meet a handsome guy?"

Molly cocked an ear.

"You do, huh?"

Molly huffed and nudged Meg with her feathery muzzle.

Meg kissed Molly's nose. It was so unfair that such magnificent animals couldn't talk to humans. Or maybe they did, and humans just weren't very good listeners.

A gunshot startled them. Molly tossed her head and stepped back.

"Easy," Meg whispered, holding her by the cheek strap. "We'll be out of here in a minute."

She led the horse out into the sunlight.

"Hey, Meg! Come try your hand at a pop can."

Her brother Jeremy and his best friend, Dex, were target practicing with tin cans lined up on a few bales of hay.

"Can't. Got to take Molly out."

Just then, one of the barn cats darted out from the stacked hay behind the targets.

Dex raised his rifle.

"Don't!" Meg shouted.

Bam!

The bullet blasted the dirt just behind the cat's tail. The

cat leaped straight up, then landed, stumbled, and raced around the side of the barn.

Dex and Jeremy laughed as Meg yelled, "What are you *doing*?"

"What?" Dex said, his hands up in surrender. "I didn't hit it."

"You're sick! You scared her half to death!"

She grabbed a hank of mane, jumped up onto Molly's bare back, and loped away.

8

Meg rode toward the arena, where Amigo was. She knew horses had a pecking order, and if that order was disturbed, things could get nasty.

But today, Meg figured it would come down to how well Molly and Amigo liked each other. Kind of like humans.

Amigo was alone in the far corner of the 160-by-100-foot arena where she'd been keeping him.

Meg loped Molly twice around the paddock, hoping to spark Amigo's curiosity.

Amigo pranced over to the fence.

Meg slowed and walked Molly toward him, pulling up close but not too close. "Amigo," she said softly. "Meet Molly Montana."

Amigo shook his head and snorted.

Molly whinnied in return.

"Well, that's good news."

Meg dismounted, took Molly over, and unhitched the gate that separated the pasture from the working pen. She pushed it open and led her horse through. Even before she could close the gate, Amigo came up to Molly. They touched noses and sniffed, huffing low and nodding.

Meg slowly reached up to touch Amigo's cheek. He

jerked his head and backed off. She cupped Molly's feathery chin. "I didn't think it would be this easy, Molly-girl. What do you know about this guy that I don't?"

Meg removed Molly's halter.

When Amigo stepped away, Molly followed him. When Amigo bent low, Molly did, as well.

"Wow," Meg whispered.

The two horses stood head to head. Amigo sniffed Molly, moving from cheek to shoulder.

Molly lazily sniffed Amigo back.

"What do you say I leave her in here for a while, Amigo?"

Amigo threw his head and raced away, then turned and pranced back, ears cocked forward. He wasn't even a shadow of the horse he was when she'd gotten him, and she'd been working hard for that.

Meg reached around Molly's chin and pulled her close. "Think you can handle being in here for a while with a guy like that?"

Amigo stopped abruptly a little ways off, as if taunting Molly to follow him.

Molly just looked at him.

"Oh, go on," Meg said, nudging her. "I think he likes you."

But Molly just bobbed over to scratch her neck on the fence.

"Guess I don't have to worry about you two."

Meg laughed, and headed back to the barn.

9

After Mr. Brodie left and Danny had finished his chores, Ricky rode up to the barn on his bike.

"Hey," Danny mumbled.

Ricky frowned. "What's up? You look like roadkill."

"Billy Brodie shot Banjo."

"*What!*"

"I can't find him. But I think he's still alive."

"How do you know he's shot?"

"Mr. Brodie came over. He said Billy winged him because he was chasing their sheep."

"No way," Ricky said. "Banjo doesn't chase sheep . . . or anything else."

"That's what I tried to tell Mr. Brodie. But he didn't believe me."

Danny filled Ricky in. His voice trembled, and he couldn't stop it. "He's gotta be holed up somewhere. I was just going out to look for him. He's not dead . . . he can't be."

Ricky spat. "Those Brodie boys live off ants and stink-bugs. I never liked either one of them."

"Ben's okay, at least when he's not around Billy."

"Maybe."

"Want to help me look?"

"Yeah. I'm supposed to pick up something for my mom . . . but that can wait. Where do you want to start?"

"The gully."

Ricky dropped his bike. "Let's go."

They ran across the pasture toward the ravine. The Macks' calves and steers looked up from where they grazed.

Ricky picked up his pace. "That crazy big one isn't going to chase us, is he?"

"We'll see."

"Comforting."

The sun was full up. Danny tugged his hat low as the two of them stumbled down the trail, slipping on loose rock and half sliding to the bottom of the gully.

"Haven't been down here since we snuck out and cooked steaks in the middle of the night," Ricky said. "We should do that again."

"Yeah," Danny said. "But first we have to find Banjo."

The cave was down around the bend, hidden from view by scrub brush and juniper. Danny and Ricky pulled the weeds back and peered into the opening.

"Banjo," Danny called. "You in there?"

"Here," Ricky said, handing him a stick. "For snakes."

Danny took the stick and, with a deep breath, slowly duckwalked into the dark cavern. Four turns and it ended. But past that last turn, the cave was flat-out pure dark. Danny's sun-filled eyes could not adjust.

He felt his way deeper, the stick shaking in his hand, praying there were no rattlers in there.

His throat burned when he heard the familiar sound of a dog panting.

"Banjo?" he whispered. "That you?"

Danny banged his elbow on the side of the cave. He reached out blindly, found the rugged wall, and inched forward on hands and knees.

When he touched something furry, he gasped. "It's me, boy. I'm here. It's okay now, it's okay."

Banjo licked Danny's hand. His fur was hot, his heart racing. He yelped when Danny's fingers touched a sticky, metallic-smelling patch.

Blood.

"Aw, man."

Danny dropped the stick and lay down in the dirt with his arm around his dog.

Banjo's trembling made Danny's heart ache. "Let's get out of here, boy." He tried to get Banjo to stand, gently prodding him, staying clear of the wound. "Come on. Let's get you home and cleaned up."

But Banjo wouldn't budge.

Danny got down closer and tried to relax so the peace of his own body would take hold in Banjo's. In a moment, Banjo struggled up. "Good boy. Let's go home."

Out in the sun, Ricky gasped at the bloody gash along Banjo's hip.

"I don't think it's as bad as it looks," Danny said. "The bullet just grazed him. It doesn't look that deep."

Banjo licked Danny's face, his tail tucked up close, guilty.

Danny's eyes watered. "You don't even know what you've done, do you?"

10

Danny and Ricky carried Banjo back to the hay shed, gave him water and food, and cleaned his wound. "He doesn't seem to be in much pain," Danny said.

"Maybe he's in shock."

"How could they shoot my dog, Ricky? That's just mean."

Ricky pressed his lips tight and shook his head. "Moles. Both of them."

Danny pulled Banjo's collar all the way around. "Where's your tag, boy? There's only the one with your name on it."

Ricky stood. "I gotta go."

Danny looked up. "Thanks for staying, Ricky."

"No problem. At least your crazy steer didn't chase us."

"Maybe next time."

Ricky grunted, grabbed his bike, and took off.

• • •

A while later, when Danny went out to dump the water he'd used to clean Banjo's wound, he saw Billy and Ben Brodie prowling around the ridge. On Mack property.

When they spotted Danny, they stopped and stared.

Danny glanced behind him, relieved to see that Banjo was out of sight.

Billy Brodie was fifteen. Ben was Danny's age and in his class at school. They'd been friends for a while but had drifted apart. He was okay, but his brother had a mean streak and made it hard for Danny to be around the Brodie house. Other than ranch life, Tyrell and Danny and the Brodie boys didn't have much in common.

Billy and Ben gazed down on Danny from the ridge, like poachers who couldn't care less about getting caught trespassing. Danny'd never cared about them being on this side of the fence . . . but it was different now.

His eyes narrowed. He wouldn't put it past Billy to take another shot at Banjo if he spotted him. He shot at any and all critters that hadn't been given a name.

Danny went back into the shed and tied Banjo up.

The Brodie boys poked around on the ridge until they spotted the steer Ricky called crazy. When it started over to them, they took off.

. . .

Later that afternoon, Danny was in the barn with Banjo, cleaning Pete's feet with a hoof pick, when he heard someone drive up. He looked out.

Dad.

"Got to hide you, boy. Hurry." He led Banjo into the tack room. "Keep quiet, okay? Don't. Bark."

Banjo's tail thumped on the floor.

"Shhh."

Danny gave him a hug, then went back out and picked up Pete's hoof.

Dad poked his head into the barn. "Danny?"

"Over here."

Dad watched Danny work. "You're getting pretty good at that."

"Done it enough."

"That you have. So how'd it go, today? The fence good and sound?"

Danny nodded.

"Perfect."

For the first time in his life, Danny felt uncomfortable around Dad. He'd never hidden something from him before. But if he didn't . . . and Mr. Brodie was right. . . .

Danny listened for Banjo. Quiet.

"Well," Dad said. "I'm going in."

A few minutes later, someone else drove up.

Mr. Brodie . . . had to be.

"This is not good," Danny whispered. Mr. Brodie must have been out by the road in his truck. Waiting for Dad.

A door thumped shut.

Then another.

Danny kept working.

A minute later, Dad called to the barn. "Danny, would you come out here?"

Danny took a deep breath and went out. His stomach tightened when he saw the county sheriff's cruiser.

They were standing in a semicircle, arms crossed—Dad,

Mr. Brodie, and the sheriff. Billy and Ben sat in the bed of their father's truck, alert as hunting dogs.

Dad looked at Danny. "You didn't tell me Harmon was over today."

"No, sir."

"Why's that?"

Danny shrugged.

Mr. Brodie shook his head.

"You find Banjo?" Dad asked.

Danny put his hands in his back pockets. He could say no to Mr. Brodie and the sheriff. But he couldn't lie to Dad.

Could he?

"Danny?"

"He's in the tack room. I got him locked up."

Mr. Brodie snorted. "At least that was smart."

"Get the dog, son," the sheriff said.

Danny brought Banjo out and stood shielding him.

Billy and Ben jumped out of the truck, Billy with a rifle. Danny tried not to look at them.

The sheriff turned to Mr. Brodie. "This the dog?"

"Yep. See where my boy grazed him?"

Danny glared at Billy.

The sheriff turned and squinted at the rifle. "Why don't you put that away, son."

Billy glanced at his dad, who tipped his head toward the truck.

Billy put the rifle away.

The sheriff bent down and called Banjo. Danny let him

come around but squatted and kept his hand hooked under Banjo's collar.

"Not such a big dog," the sheriff said, letting Banjo sniff his hand. "You'd never take him for a sheep killer looking at him, would you?"

"That's because he's not a sheep killer," Danny said. "There's just no way."

Mr. Brodie said, "Don't matter what he looks like, Sheriff. That dog was chasing down my young sheep. Billy and Ben saw it. That right, boys?"

"He was chasing a ewe right across the hillside," Ben said. "Him and a bunch of wild dogs. Billy shot and clipped him. We scared the others off, right, Billy? He might have hit another one, too. I heard a squeal."

Billy nodded. "That's right."

"Banjo doesn't chase sheep," Danny pleaded. "And how do you know he wasn't chasing the other dogs off?"

Billy grunted. "He was with 'em. That's all you need to know."

Danny glanced at Dad, then away. Dad looked grim.

"I'm not here to see anyone shoot your dog," the sheriff said. "But I am here to enforce the law. Mr. Brodie's charging this dog with attacking his sheep. I have no choice but to impound him. I'm sorry."

Danny looked at Dad, wanting to yell: *Don't let them take him!*

"Dad—"

Dad raised a hand. "How long have we been living here, Danny?"

What kind of question was that? They'd never lived any-where else.

"All your life," Dad said. "And in all that time what have we done about wild dogs and coyotes that chase down our livestock?"

Danny held Banjo close. "We shoot them. But Banjo—"

Dad stopped him again. "Maybe you need to thank Billy for not shooting clean and killing him, like he could've. There's a humane way to put a wayward animal down, and they've given you that choice."

Silence.

Ben's eyes darted between Danny, the sheriff, and Billy.

No way they'd meant to spare Banjo, Danny thought. They just can't shoot straight.

Mr. Brodie softened. "Livestock come first, Danny. You know that."

Danny didn't know what to say. His hands trembled. Banjo was being tried and convicted, right here, right now, and he was the only witness against five judges who'd al-ready decided his guilt.

"I'm not here to kill your dog, son," the sheriff said. "Only to impound him."

"For how long?"

The sheriff shrugged. "Weeks. Months. If he's guilty, well, you may never see him again."

"No," Danny said. "You can't do this. He's a ranch dog. He'll die in a cage. It's cruel, it's—"

"Put him down, then," Mr. Brodie said. "More humane than a cage, anyway."

Danny started to fight back, but nothing came out. It was all too *insane*. Yesterday Banjo was running squirrels off and following him around as he did his chores. And now . . .

Danny knelt and pulled Banjo close. "No," he whispered. "No."

No one spoke for a long moment.

Dad turned to Mr. Brodie. "I have to agree with Danny. This dog won't do well caged up waiting to die. We'll take him to the vet and have him euthanized in the next day or two, if that's okay with you, Harmon."

Mr. Brodie nodded. "That'll be fine, Ray."

"Well, then," the sheriff said. He shook hands with the two men and left. The Brodies climbed into their truck and followed the sheriff out.

Dad turned to Danny. "You should've told me the minute I got home."

"Yes, sir."

"Why didn't you?"

"I don't know."

"I guess this explains the gunshots you and Tyrell heard in the middle of the night."

Danny studied the dirt.

Inside the house, Dad called the vet down in Redmond. "Two days, Danny. Be sure you keep him tied up till then. We can be with him when they do it."

"This is wrong, Dad. Wrong! Banjo's no sheep killer. You *know* that."

"Thought I did. But it seems that's not the case." He sighed. "We don't have a choice. I'd expect the same of Harmon if it were the other way around."

"But *kill* him? Why can't I can find him a home or give him to somebody?"

"Not up to me, son."

"Why?"

"Harmon's pressed charges. The law will take him, and unless we want to hire a lawyer and try to fight it, he'll probably be put down."

"Then let's hire a lawyer."

Dad shook his head. "Be a waste of money we don't have."

"But—"

"That's my decision, Danny. Nothing more to it."

Banjo settled down in the dirt, looking up at them, his wet tongue jiggling as he panted in the heat.

Danny's chest felt tight, his breathing shallow. "Let me have one more week with him, Dad, just one more week. Call the vet and change it."

"Don't prolong it. It will only hurt you more."

"I don't care. I just want one more week!"

Maybe he could find a way to make the whole thing disappear. Find someone to take Banjo in. Then he'd just tell Dad and Mr. Brodie that Banjo ran away or something. He probably couldn't find him a home anywhere around here, though. He'd have to tell people why he was giving Banjo up, and that would kill the deal with everyone he knew.

Maybe Ricky would take him. His family didn't own livestock.

But they lived near people who did.

Dad put a hand on Danny's shoulder. "We agreed to two days, and we have to stick with that."

Danny spurted, "No!"

"Danny—"

"I'll do it myself."

Silence.

Dad studied him. "You'd shoot him?"

"Y . . . yes."

Danny turned away, wondering where those awful words had come from.

11

When Tyrell drove home from work, Danny ran out to meet him. He could barely stand still. "I found Banjo!" he said before Tyrell even got out of the truck.

"Where was he?"

"The cave in the gully. Billy Brodie shot him. That's what the shots we heard were all about. They said—"

"Whoa, slow down. Billy Brodie *shot* Banjo?"

"He could've killed him, Tyrell."

"But why?"

"Mr. Brodie said Banjo was attacking their sheep with a pack of wild dogs. He came blazing over to ask me what I was going to do about it. Just after Dad left this morning. I didn't know what to say. But he wanted Banjo put down."

Danny told Tyrell how the sheriff and Dad and Mr. Brodie stood around talking about how and when to get it done. "Dad told Mr. Brodie we'd have Banjo put down in two days."

"What? That's crazy." Tyrell got out and slammed the door.

Danny glanced toward the house. He had to talk fast.

"Dad made a deal with Mr. Brodie. You know he doesn't go back on his word."

Tyrell nodded.

Danny paused. *Just say it.* "I told Dad I'd shoot him myself."

Tyrell stopped and gaped at him.

"There's no way any of this is going to happen," Danny added. "Banjo's innocent. I know it and you do, too. In all the time we've had him he hasn't even chased a barn cat."

"We don't have any barn cats."

"You know what I mean."

Tyrell crossed his arms. "So, Banjo is . . . where?"

"In the hay shed, tied up."

They stood a moment.

"Banjo didn't do it, Tyrell."

"Problem is," Tyrell said, "Billy and Ben can say anything they want. It's their word against nobody's."

"Do you think Spike can take Banjo?" Danny asked. Spike worked with Tyrell at his job. "I know he likes dogs, and he's not a rancher."

"I can ask, but he'll say no."

"Why?"

"His wife is still broken up about losing their dog, Grouch."

"Ask anyway, okay? If I don't find him a home, he'll die."

Tyrell nodded.

"All I know is nobody's killing my dog."

"I'll ask everyone I know," Tyrell said. "But that's not a whole lot of people who aren't from around here." He tapped Danny's back. "C'mon, man. I'm starving."

12

FRIDAY

On the morning after Mr. Brodie and the sheriff had come to Danny's place, Meg Harris headed out to see Amigo with a soft halter tucked into her back pocket, out of sight. Amigo would notice. He saw everything. She knew she wouldn't get it on him, but she wanted him to see it so he wouldn't be scared of it later.

He was waiting for her at the gate. First time he'd ever done that. "Well, look at you. Missing me?"

Then she got it. "Ah, you want to see Molly again."

Meg approached slowly. "I'll bring her out, but not right now."

Amigo eyed her, his head high and alert.

"You're looking very handsome," she said.

The nicks and scars were gone now. His coat was no longer dull, and his ribs had filled out. As soon as Amigo trusted her enough to get close, and stay close, she could brush the tangles out of his mane and tail.

When she opened the gate to enter the pen, he whinnied and took off, tail high.

For weeks now, Meg had been giving him feed in a large

tin pan she placed on the ground in the pen, just enough to fill him up. She'd fill the pan and walk away, and Amigo would trot over and nose it up.

When he got hungry again, Meg would be there to give him just a little more. She hoped that this would help him see that a human wasn't something to move away from, but toward.

Now, Amigo was circling the pen.

Meg walked in and closed the gate.

Amigo snorted and tossed his head, bulging eye watching her. It took some courage to ignore him, but ignoring him was what raised his curiosity. Even harder was turning her back on him. But she had to trust that he would do her no harm.

Slowly he ventured closer to see what she was up to.

Each time Meg moved away, Amigo followed.

She hummed as she walked, ignoring him. She could hear him behind her, coming close, then circling away and returning.

When, in a while, he came up behind her and nudged her with his muzzle, Meg froze and covered her mouth with her hand . . . then smiled.

13

That same morning, Tyrell drove Danny into the country west of their ranch. Banjo sat on Danny's lap, nose out the window and ears flapping in the wind.

The night before, Danny had called every kid he knew from school, begging them to take Banjo. But none of them could, or would. Ricky wanted to take him, but when his dad asked why Danny was giving his dog away, Ricky had to tell him.

"Sorry, Danny," Ricky said. "My dad won't risk it. I called three other guys I know, and their parents said the same thing. Can't you find him a home in Bend? Or better, somewhere they don't have livestock, like Eugene or Portland?"

"Don't have time. And I don't know anyone there."

"You really told your dad you'd shoot your own dog?"

Danny closed his eyes. "I had to think of something."

"Oh, man . . . now what?

When Danny didn't answer, Ricky said, "Don't tell me you're *really* going to shoot him."

"Worse."

"How's that possible?"

Danny told him.

"I don't think I could do that," Ricky said.

"Maybe I can't, either."

Now, as Tyrell drove out into the country, Danny's thoughts were like barbed wire in his brain. He shut his eyes and tugged his hat down low, trying hard not to think about the Winchester in the window rack behind him.

He looked in the side-view mirror, but it was cracked and pointing toward the sky. Danny reached out and tried to adjust it.

"Broken," Tyrell said. "I need to get a new one."

"What'd you do to it?"

"Some idiot hit it with a baseball bat, or something. While I was at work. Got five more cars, too." He shook his head. "Fools everywhere."

Danny pulled Banjo closer. "Did you ask Spike?"

Tyrell nodded. "He said his wife isn't ready for another dog."

Danny closed his eyes and threw his head back.

"Don't think about it," Tyrell said. "It'll drive you nuts."

"Already has."

They drove in silence, country fence posts slipping by. Danny slapped the seat. "Come on, Tyrell, we have to know *someone* who can take him."

"Not a chance. Maybe Portland, but who do we know there? We don't even have time to put an ad in the paper. Where exactly are we going, anyway?"

"Camp Sherman, I guess."

"What's out there?"

"Forest."

Tyrell turned to look at Danny. "We ain't seen nothing *but* forest. Why out there?"

"It's faraway forest."

Minutes later they were beyond Sisters, heading toward the mountain pass. The sun was straight up and hot.

"I don't know about this," Tyrell said. "I mean, is it more humane to euthanize him or turn him loose? He's a pet. He doesn't know how to live in the wild."

Danny looked out his window.

Tyrell turned the radio on.

"All I know is nobody's killing Banjo." Danny turned the radio off. Music was wrong at a time like this.

Tyrell looked at him, then back at the road.

When they reached the turnoff for Camp Sherman, they headed to where the Metolius River ran cold and clear. They pulled up and parked in front of Camp Sherman's one store, a shoebox among the giant ponderosa pines.

Danny opened the door.

Banjo started to jump out with him, but Danny held him back.

"Stay."

Banjo sat. He'd always been a good dog.

Just outside the store, two men wearing baseball caps sat on a bench with their arms crossed over their large bellies. "Ask them if they want a dog," Danny said, low.

"You go on in," Tyrell said, and sat on the bench with the two men. "Either of you gents want a dog?"

Inside, Danny bought two bottles of water and a packet of beef jerky, then went out and nodded to Tyrell.

Tyrell stood. "Nice talking with ya."

They got back in the truck and followed the road down-river.

"Well?" Danny asked.

"Nope."

"Did they even consider it?"

"For about a second."

Danny closed his eyes, his chest tight.

Three miles later they parked in a dirt pullout near the river. The dry air smelled like mint.

Danny let Banjo out. "Go on and run a bit."

He tossed Tyrell a bottle of water and jammed the other one and the jerky into his back pockets.

Moments later Banjo came loping out of the brush. Danny knelt and scratched his ears, which Banjo liked, his eyes closing to slits.

Danny hugged him for a long time, then got up and reached into the truck for the rifle.

They headed downriver.

Soon they crossed a bridge and angled into the trees on the other side, looking for a place where campers or fisher-men or hikers would not go.

Tyrell trailed Danny. "You know where you're going?"

"No."

"We could get lost in here."

"Long as we can hear the river, we're good."

They kept the river within earshot, though the sound grew weaker. When they stopped, Banjo was somewhere deep in the woods.

Tyrell sat and leaned against a tree. "Why'd you tell Dad you were going to put Banjo down when you knew that would never happen?"

"To keep him alive."

Tyrell snorted. "Now, there's irony for you."

Danny sat and laid the rifle in the pine needles. They waited in the eerie silence of motionless trees. When Banjo finally came back, he lay down next to them, tongue out, panting.

Danny's head started to throb.

He looked at the rifle. "This is the worst day of my life."

Tyrell tossed a rock into the thick trees. "Just do it and let's go home."

Danny reached over and put a hand on Banjo's head. "I'm sorry, Banjo . . . I . . . I . . ."

There were no words.

Banjo's ears perked forward, his eyes bright.

Danny ripped open the packet of jerky with his teeth and held out a piece.

Banjo snapped it up and started gnawing on it.

"That's not going to help us do what we came here to do," Tyrell said. When Danny didn't answer, Tyrell closed his eyes. "Time to get serious."

Danny rubbed his temples. How long could he put it off? He took the bottle of water and poured some into his cupped hand. Banjo lapped it up.

Please, God, help me, because I can't do this by myself.

He gave Banjo more water, then hugged him so tight

Banjo yelped. Danny let up but couldn't let go. He buried his head in Banjo's black and white fur.

"Oh, for Pete's sake!"

Tyrell pushed himself up, grabbed the Winchester, raised it to his cheek, and aimed.

14

After her amazing morning with Amigo, Meg took Molly out for a ride in the forest. "Let's go find us a place where the only thing you can hear is the breeze, what do you say, Molly-girl?"

Heading out into wild country settled her mind. The riding felt easy, as if land and animal joined up to remind her that life was much more than it seemed when you were around people.

People.

Like Dex, who'd shoot at a cat.

What was it that made him so thoughtless?

She rode through the old pines, following a trail toward the mountains. The freedom she felt out here nearly brought tears to her eyes.

Tears?

Where were these feelings coming from?

In her mind she heard an old Hank Williams song.

I'm so lonesome I could cry.

Loneliness?

Maybe.

Why was that? Maybe she was just too weird for most people. How many thirteen-year-olds had the notion that they could talk to horses? And what about birds? How could she ever explain the feeling of sitting perfectly still overlooking a river, wondering what it would be like to fly, to be a hawk or an eagle, hanging in the air on barely moving wings?

Meg rode into a field of wildflowers at the base of the mountains.

She wiped her eyes. Maybe it was Amigo and the way he was starting to trust her. Maybe it was just relief at having that 4-H demonstration over!

She missed Josie. She'd understand. But she and her family had gone to Alaska on vacation right after the demonstration. They were on a boat. Meg couldn't even call her.

But Meg still had her brothers. She smiled, thinking of them sitting like fence posts at her demonstration. Not every girl had brothers who showed up like that.

Jacob, a state-ranked quarterback, would be a senior at Sisters High. He was her favorite brother. Of course she liked Jeremy, too, just not in the same way. Jacob was the one who always watched out for her.

On the field, he was as savage as the other guys. He was nearly ten inches taller than she was. But inside, where the real Jacob lived, he was calm and kind-hearted.

Meg pulled up and took a sip from her canteen. She leaned over and ran her hand down Molly's warm neck. "Doing okay, girl?"

Molly turned an ear and bent low to rip up a hank of dry grass.

Then she raised her head, both ears cocked forward.

Meg was instantly alert.

Black bears, cougars, and rattlesnakes were often seen in this country. But Molly wasn't displaying the fear that a bear or cougar would inspire.

"What is it, Mol? Something out there?"

Meg turned to listen.

Only the wind combing through the trees.

But Molly, her ears still pinned forward, hadn't moved a twitch.

Someone, or some*thing*, was out there.

15

Tyrell fired, the bullet thwacking through the trees. He fired again, aiming high, shouldering past Danny toward Banjo.

Banjo staggered back, crouching, ears flat, eyes wild.

Tyrell fired again and again into the trees just above Banjo's head. Banjo stumbled, turned, and fled.

Tyrell kept following, firing and firing.

Until Banjo disappeared.

16

Crack!

Molly shied, and Meg reined in abruptly, hearing the shot.

One, two, three.

Then two more.

Not close . . . but not far, either.

Maybe close enough to catch a stray bullet. She quickly pulled Molly behind the biggest tree she could find.

When the shooting stopped, Meg moved out, moving closer to the gunshots. Why, she didn't know. It wasn't wise.

Molly slid down a dusty, loose rock gully and lurched up the other side.

Meg reined in to listen.

Everything was still, like in the deep of night.

Spooky.

After a long moment, she and Molly headed home.

17

By the time Danny and Tyrell passed back through Sisters on their way home, the sun was setting.

Usually, Danny enjoyed this drive. But this time he stared at the passing trees with glazed eyes, leaning against the passenger door, one boot up on the dash. It had happened so fast, so final. Tyrell doing what he couldn't. Danny didn't know whether to thank him or kick him.

What would he tell Dad? That he'd shot his own dog? Or would he tell him the truth?

He wanted to punch something. *You creep! You don't abandon your dog!*

Tyrell slowed as they turned and headed up the dusty road to their house.

Danny looked at him.

"What?" Tyrell said.

"Don't you feel bad about Banjo?"

"Sure, but what else could we have done? No one around here is going to take a dog that chases livestock. And neither of us could ever shoot him. What was left to do?"

"Maybe we could've secretly taken him to the Humane Society."

"Maybe. But we didn't."

Tyrell rolled up his window against the dust off the dirt road. "So what are we going to tell Dad?"

"I don't know yet." Danny frowned.

The truth?

Or . . . a lie?

How could he do either?

They pulled up and parked next to Dad's truck.

Tyrell tapped Danny's knee. "Whatever it is you tell him . . . well . . . we're in this together now."

Danny nodded.

They got out. Danny looked back at the rifle. He slammed the door shut. He didn't want to touch it.

Tyrell reached in and got it.

Dad was sitting at the kitchen table with his checkbook and a handful of bills, listening to the radio. He looked up. "You boys took your time."

Danny turned away. He couldn't look at him. He would know.

Tyrell headed to the fridge.

Danny took off his hat and ran his fingers through his hair. He wanted to run back to Camp Sherman.

Banjo. Terrified. Alone.

What had he *done*?

18

In the barn, Meg unsaddled Molly, brushed her down, and walked her out back. Late-afternoon tree shadows spiked over the pasture. Meg turned Molly out and breathed in the sweet aroma of horses and hay.

But the shots . . . so many shots.

Poachers?

It was hard to let go of the sound echoing through the trees.

She remembered the way Molly had stood, perfectly still, ears cocked forward, as if she'd heard or seen something even before it happened.

Tomorrow Meg would go back and have a look around.

Maybe she'd find what it was.

Or it would find her.

19

The scratchy army blanket on Danny's bed was tucked and cornered tight, military style. Dad had taught him to make it the way he had in the Marines.

Danny stood in the doorway and stared at it in a daze.

He went in and closed the door quietly, took off his shirt, and sat on his bed holding it.

A moment later, there was a quiet knock on his door.

"It's not locked," Danny said.

Dad opened it and leaned against the door frame. "Hungry?"

Danny shook his head.

Dad looked at the rodeo posters on Danny's wall. "I might be able to pick you up another one of these over in Durango. I'm passing through in a couple of weeks."

Danny tossed his shirt across the room into the plastic laundry basket. Dad came in and sat next to him. "How you feeling?"

"Kind of horse kicked." An understatement.

"Where'd you boys take him?"

Danny took his time answering. "Over near Camp Sherman."

"Did he suffer?"

"No."

Just like that. Made up his mind even before he said it. A lie.

He closed his eyes and shook his head.

"I'm sorry, Danny, I truly am."

Danny said nothing.

"What'd you do with him . . . after?"

Danny hadn't thought about that. "Uh . . . we buried him. I took a shovel."

Another lie.

"Just where you shot him?"

"Y-yes, sir."

"Don't know if that's legal."

Danny said nothing.

"Well, anyway, it's done and I'm truly sorry it came to this. I honestly didn't think that dog would go after stock. Never had before."

Danny could hear the radio out in the kitchen, a rollicking country song. It sounded way out of place.

"Sure you're not hungry?"

"I don't think I could eat for a week."

"Well, don't forget the horses."

"I'll do it now."

Danny stood and picked up his hat, then put it back down. It was getting dark out and he didn't need it. Still, he felt naked without it. He put it on.

Dad pushed himself up. "I know it wasn't easy." He paused, then added, "That had to have been the hardest thing you've ever done."

"I think I'm going to sleep in the hay shed tonight."

Dad nodded, squeezed Danny's shoulder, and left.

Danny put his shirt back on and went out and called the horses to the feeder. He forked in some hay and alfalfa as they came up from a dark corner, one after the other. When he was done he got his sleeping bag and took it out to the hay shed. He lay where Banjo slept, hands behind his head.

There were times when Danny really wished he had someone to talk to, someone he could open up to. Like his mom. Say what he felt.

But she'd worry and get all over Dad.

This was his problem, and he'd deal with it.

In the middle of the night, Danny rolled up his sleeping bag and headed back to the house. Sleeping in the shed without Banjo was worse than pitching a tent in a cemetery.

At the front door he stopped and looked back.

Somewhere out there a hungry dog wandered in the wild, betrayed by the one he'd loved and trusted most.

20

SATURDAY

The next morning, Meg got up and went about her chores, and it wasn't until the afternoon that she rode again into the pines, Molly huffing, saddle leather creaking.

Every few minutes she stopped to listen and look for signs that she was retracing the trail she'd taken the day before.

She stopped to eat an apple as Molly drank from a clear stream. All signs of civilization had faded. She was close to where she'd heard the shots. Close enough to spook her. Had the shooters camped overnight? Were they out there crouching in the weeds in their camo jackets, watching her ride past?

Meg clicked her tongue, and Molly moved on.

Every flick of movement in the corner of Meg's eye made her stomach leap. "We're getting close, Molly-girl," she whispered.

Molly cocked one ear back.

They came to a familiar meadow where long grasses brushed the bottom of Meg's boots as she rode through it.

As they approached the trees on the other side, Molly shied to the right.

Meg pulled up and bent over her neck. "Easy now, easy."

This is the place.

Like yesterday, there was nothing unusual about the trees and the meadow. Nothing in the brush, the grass, the rocks.

Standing in the stirrups and looking back, Meg saw only their trail through the long grass. Ahead, the pine forest loomed behind a line of white-barked aspens.

She clucked Molly on, and stood again in the stirrups when Molly stopped and raised her head. There . . . just ahead in the aspens.

A shadow.

No . . . not a shadow.

Something dead . . . or alive.

Molly threw her head and sidestepped.

"Easy."

Meg tried to get a better look, knowing not to approach without more information. Could be a small black bear.

But a bear would be loping off by now.

Molly was too jumpy. Meg dismounted and led her closer.

There. Under a tree.

"What the heck . . . A dog?"

21

Meg knelt near the black-and-white dog.

It was alive. She could see it breathing. Its eyes were open, but they seemed almost vacant. Was it sick?

Meg looked up, figuring she was probably about three or four miles from Camp Sherman, too far for someone's dog to have wandered off.

She didn't see a campsite. No hikers, no one calling their dog. It was a pet, she could tell that much. A wild one would be long gone at the sight of her. Not this one.

Molly stretched forward to see.

The dog peeked up but didn't raise its head.

"What are you doing way out here?" Meg said.

Its eyes shifted to hers.

Meg reached out to offer her scent. A small swirl of flies circled the dog's eyes, making it wink.

Meg turned toward the sun. She should start heading home. Her mom would worry if she came in too late. But she couldn't just leave the dog. "You want to come home with me?"

There was a long shallow cut on its hip. She could see that it had bled but wasn't bleeding now. Maybe it got hit by a car on the highway and dragged itself way out here to heal, or die. But the highway was miles away.

She pulled her hand back. What if it had rabies? Or something else?

Meg glimpsed a piece of what looked like a collar and reached in and felt a metal tag. "Well, at least now we know how to find who you belong to."

No address and no phone number.

Just a name.

"Banjo," she said.

22

Meg stood and slapped her thighs. "Come on, Banjo. Get up. You can come home with me."

The dog blinked. Flies rose and circled and settled back down to drink again from its eyes.

Meg frowned. She'd never seen a dog so unresponsive. "I can't carry you. Come on, now. Get up and follow me home. It's not far."

Maybe it was injured in a way she couldn't see. A broken leg? She sighed. "Okay, listen. I'll be back soon. I'm going for help."

Molly sidestepped as Meg tried to get her foot in the stirrup. "It's okay, girl," she said softly.

She grabbed the pommel and swung up. She took a last look at the dog and hurried off. It wasn't the first dog she'd come across in the woods, but it was the first one that wouldn't even try to get up.

Thirty minutes later she dusted down the trail that led to a gravel road, where she nearly ran into a pickup truck.

Molly lunged sideways and almost sent Meg up and over her head.

The truck swerved off the road and slid to a stop.

Meg bent over Molly's neck to calm her, though her

own heart thundered from the scare. "Whoa, girl. It's okay, it's okay."

Their neighbor Ben Carter poked his head out the window. "Meg Harris, I almost got you. Where you running off to?"

"Home. I need to get Dad."

"Something wrong?"

"I found a dog."

"Where?"

"Out there, way out."

"Injured?"

"Can't really tell. He won't get up."

"Is it wild?"

"No."

"Whose is it?"

"I don't know."

"Don't get near it if it's sick. Could be rabid."

"That's why I'm getting Dad."

"Better tell him to bring a sidearm case he's got to put it out of its misery."

Meg hadn't thought of that. "I'll tell him."

"Slow down before you hurt somebody."

As he drove off, Meg thought, The last thing I'm telling Dad is to bring his gun.

23

The sky was gray blue when Meg loped up to the house in the final hours of daylight. Time was short. In the dark, she'd never find the dog again.

Dad's truck wasn't there.

"Not good," she said as she slipped off Molly. He and her brothers were probably practicing for football at the high school. She'd have to find a way to do it herself.

"Meg!" Mom called from the barn.

Meg turned. "Mom, I need help!"

"Where've you been? I was starting to worry."

"I found a dog. He won't get up. He's way out in the woods."

"Is he hurt?"

"It's on his side. I don't know whose dog it is, but he needs help."

Mom thought for a moment. "Saddle Sunspot. I'll leave a note and fill a canteen. Dad and the boys won't be back for a couple of hours."

Meg led Molly into the barn and saddled Mom's horse.

Minutes later they headed into the trees riding single file, Meg leading. In the meadows, they rode side by side, racing the fading light.

Meg found Banjo by following the trail she'd left coming out. "There. Just where I left him."

They dismounted and hunched down to look at him. "There's a tag. See? His name is Banjo."

Mom reached out to let the dog sniff her hand. Banjo opened his eyes, but that was all. Mom stroked his head, then felt along his back, ribs, and legs. When she came to Banjo's flesh wound, he looked up and nipped the air.

"Looks like he's got a cut of some kind on his hip," she said. "Get the canteen. Let's see if he'll drink some water."

Meg got the water and poured some into her hand.

Banjo sniffed it and turned away.

"I tried to get him to come home with me, but he wouldn't move. Wouldn't even lift his head. Why's he like this, Mom?"

Mom stroked Banjo's neck.

"Could be anything. Maybe somebody drove him far from home and abandoned him. People get rid of unwanted pets that way."

"That's sick, Mom."

"I'm not saying that's what happened, but it's possible."

"Who would do something like that?"

"You'd be surprised."

Mom sat back on her heels. "You know what I think?"

"He came out here to die?"

"Something like that, but no. Look at him. Look at those eyes. This dog has a broken heart."

24

It took gentle patience for Mom to lift Banjo across Meg's lap as she sat in her saddle. Banjo nipped her when she touched his grazed hip, just to warn. He had yet to make a sound.

It was twilight by the time they got home. Mom carried Banjo into the barn and settled him onto a folded blanket that Meg placed on a bed of hay in an empty horse stall.

"This dog has been traumatized," Mom said, putting a hand on Banjo's head. "You poor thing."

Meg's eyes began to water.

Mom stood and hugged her. "You okay out here by yourself? I have to start dinner."

Meg nodded, wiping her eyes with her fingers.

"Don't forget the horses."

"I won't."

Meg brought Molly and Sunspot in and quickly unsaddled them. She brushed them down and turned them out for the night. On the way back in she filled a tin bowl with water and set it by Banjo.

Banjo didn't even look at it.

Meg sat down next to him and picked the burrs out of

his coat. "I like your name, Banjo. Who gave it to you? And where'd you come from?"

She bent close to look at him. Eyes can tell you so much, but what she saw in Banjo's was a dying campfire.

"I know!" Meg jumped to her feet and clapped. "Come on, boy, let's run around the barn, come on."

Banjo lifted his head, startled.

"That's it, come on! Get up!"

He settled back down and looked up at her.

Meg leaned forward, her hands on her knees. "Well, I'm not giving up on you, so you can just forget about that."

Maybe she'd sleep out here tonight.

In the yard, truck doors slammed. The door to the house creaked open. Minutes later, her dad and two brothers came out to the barn and stood around her. "Mom says you found a dog," Dad said.

Jacob squatted and looked Banjo over.

Meg reached for his tag. "His name is Banjo. No other information."

"Where'd you find him?"

"Little bit northeast of Camp Sherman."

"What were you doing out there?" Dad asked.

"Just riding. Mom thinks someone abandoned him."

Jacob scratched under Banjo's chin. "Hey, dog. Somebody dump you?"

Banjo wouldn't look at him directly.

Jeremy clicked his tongue. "I find out who dumped this dog, I'll take a whip to him."

Dad put a hand on Jeremy's arm.

"Sorry."

Dad hunched down and felt around Banjo's body. He stopped when Banjo winced. "How bad's the wound?"

"Not too," Meg said.

Dad looked closer. "Looks like he was grazed by a bullet."

"What!" Jeremy barked.

"He's okay," Dad added. "At least physically."

"Mom thinks he has a broken heart."

Dad frowned and pushed himself up. "Time for dinner, Meg."

Meg sighed. "I'll be back, sad dog," she said. "I'll take care of you. Don't you worry about anything."

25

SUNDAY

Tyrell had a summer job at Les Schwab Tire Center in Sisters, so most of the chores were left to Danny. Which was fine with him, because the only thing that seemed to help keep his mind off Banjo was work.

He tossed hay and alfalfa into the horse feeders, mucked out the stalls, spread new wood chips, and headed out to the pasture with a wheelbarrow full of manure that he unloaded near a stubborn old stump they'd been trying to dig out, attacking it with picks and shovels.

Dad was at the gate resetting a hinge. "Been thinking," he called over to Danny. "How 'bout you, me, and Tyrell haul the horses on down to Harney County one day this week? I can take some time off. We can ride up Steens Mountain and see if we can't get your mind off that dog."

Danny set the wheelbarrow down. "Uh, well . . . this Saturday's the rodeo, and I've got to . . . you know. Get ready. Practice."

The last thing he wanted to do was spend hours in a truck talking about Banjo. "Besides, Tyrell works weekdays."

Dad paused, looking at Danny. "I'm sorry you had to do

what you did to your dog. Real sorry." Then, softly, "I know it wasn't easy."

Danny stared at his boots. What could he say? He nodded and moved on, the wheelbarrow wobbling over the uneven ground.

He probably could have told his mom the truth about Banjo. She'd have understood. Maybe. He'd thought again of calling her but couldn't do it.

He wanted to tell the truth. But the truth would only make it worse. It would expose how he'd lied and deceived his dad, the sheriff, and Mr. Brodie. And the whole world would know that he'd abandoned his dog. Worse, the truth would get Banjo locked up.

No, he couldn't say anything. At least out in the wild, Banjo had a chance.

Maybe.

Danny looked over at the stump. He'd start on that next. Hack on it until his hands bled. There wasn't enough work in the world to make him stop thinking about Banjo.

26

Just before dawn the next morning, Danny crept into his brother's room. "Tyrell," he whispered. "Wake up. We gotta go."

Tyrell had to be at work by ten. They didn't have a lot of time.

"Huh? Oh." Tyrell sat up and rubbed his face. "Give me five."

The night before, Danny had talked Tyrell and Ricky into going back out to Camp Sherman. Guilt was driving him crazy. He had to fix things . . . without Dad and Mr. Brodie knowing. If he could get Banjo back, he would hide him somewhere and move mountains to find a home for him.

The sky was just starting to lighten, the road empty of cars.

Ricky was sitting on his heels at the end of his driveway.

Danny opened the door and slid over. "Hey," he said. "Thanks for coming."

Ricky got in. "Kind of a late start, don't you think?"

Tyrell grunted.

They drove on without speaking.

Danny couldn't help searching the trees along the way, thinking about all the things he could have done for Banjo, like having Tyrell drive him to Portland or the Humane Society in Bend. *Stupid, stupid, stupid! You could have done that!*

"You know that steer of yours?" Ricky said. "The crazy one?"

Danny turned to look at him. "What?"

"The crazy steer, the one looks like he's going to come out and stomp you but never does?"

"What are you talking about?"

"Think I could ride him? I mean, would your dad care?"

Tyrell laughed. "Now there's an oddball question."

"How can you think of that at a time like this?" Danny said.

"I bet he'd buck like his tail was on fire."

Danny shook his head. "Jeez."

They rode the rest of the way in silence, first to Camp Sherman Store, then downriver to where Danny and Tyrell had left the truck the last time.

"We walk from here," Danny said, his heart thumping. What if they found him dead?

"Haven't been out here in a while," Ricky said, glancing around. "Why do you think he's still here? Wouldn't he have run off, maybe looking for a way home or for food?"

Tyrell sighed. "I told him this was a waste of time."

"He's here," Danny said, his hands on his hips. "Somewhere . . . out there."

They made their way through the trees to the spot where

they'd chased him off. "Let's get this over with," Tyrell said. "Break up and meet back at the river in an hour. Good?"

They found nothing.

Danny lagged behind as they headed back to the truck. He didn't even have the will to punch a tree or throw a rock. His anger was gone. In its place was just a hole that good things fell into and vanished.

They stopped at the Camp Sherman store, where Danny tacked up a note on the information board, asking if anyone had found or seen a black-and-white dog.

Ricky read the other notices. "Don't forget your phone number."

"Yeah." Danny added the number and posted the note with a thumbtack he took off the corner of someone else's.

Then he ripped it down.

"Why'd you do that?" Ricky asked.

"What if someone finds him and calls the house and Dad answers?"

"Right. He thinks you shot him."

"And what are we going to tell him when we get home?" Tyrell said. "He's gonna want to know why we weren't there when he got up."

Danny crumpled the note. "I'll think of something."

27

"Well," Dad said when Tyrell and Danny got back. He was in the barn with Mandingo. "Where'd you two run off to so early this morning?"

"Black Butte," Danny said, a bit too fast. "Tyrell drove me halfway up, then I fast-climbed to the top on foot. I thought it would help me get warmed up for . . . for Saturday's rodeo . . . you know?"

That was pretty thin.

Dad nodded.

"I got to get ready for work," Tyrell said, and headed for the house.

Dad bent over, reached around the back of Mandingo's leg, and ran his hand down the inside. "Come on." He tugged lightly for Mandingo to lift his foot.

He cupped his hand around the hoof wall. "You could've just run down to Redmond and back."

"I thought working in a higher altitude would be better."

The lies just keep pouring out.

Dad picked out a clod of dirt from around the shoe and dropped Mandingo's leg.

"I . . . I need to build up my endurance," Danny added.

Dad moved to the hind leg.

Danny avoided his eyes. *He knows something's not right.*

He was just about to back away and leave when Dad said, "You think the dog will affect your roping?"

"N-no. I can do it."

"Two horns this time?"

"Two or I quit." In their last event Danny had only roped one, and that had cost them points.

"Been practicing on the dummy?"

"Every day . . . almost."

"If you want to be a winner, you got to get rid of the almost part."

Danny nodded and started to leave.

"Did you put rocks over the grave so's he won't get dug up?"

Danny winced, his eyes darting from Dad to the ground. "Yeah."

"Something more on your mind?"

Danny glanced over, then quickly away. "No."

"You can talk to me, son. You know that. When you keep things inside, they tend to get worse."

"Yes, sir."

Dad looked at Danny, waiting for more.

When nothing came, he put a hand on Mandingo's shoulder and said, "There's one good thing come out of all of this. It's taught you how to be brave when things get tough."

Danny winced and peeked back at Dad. He thought he looked tired, or sad.

"Dad, I . . . I gotta go. Tyrell said I could, you know . . . hang out with him today."

28

Danny caught Tyrell just as he was heading out to go to work. "Can I come with you today?"

"Right now?"

"Yeah. Can I go with you? I told Dad you said I could."

Tyrell grinned. "Boy, you're really spinning the tall tales, aren't you?"

Danny looked away. "If I stay here, I'll go crazy."

"There's always the stump."

"I'm serious, Tyrell, come on."

"Fine. Can't hurt to get your hands dirty."

Tyrell grabbed the keys to his truck off a table by the door. "I don't feel so good about what we did, either. Let's get out of here."

"He didn't do it, Tyrell. He doesn't chase sheep. That's the truth."

Tyrell grunted. "The truth is getting fuzzier by the day, ain't it?"

Danny felt heat rise in his face. But Tyrell had a point.

Tyrell's job wasn't the cleanest. But fixing flats and changing tires paid him enough for payments on his truck and some for college savings.

All the guys who worked there treated Danny like a little brother. Once in a while they even let him work alongside them. At five foot eight, Danny was big enough. If he could throw a steer, he could lift a truck tire.

Ann worked in the front office. She was nineteen and had taken a liking to Tyrell, and everybody there knew it. The funny part was that Tyrell didn't have a clue as to what to do about it. Whenever Ann came up and hooked her arm under his, he went quiet. Ann liked Danny, too. "I wish I had brothers like you guys," she said once. "Mine don't even talk to each other."

It was a quiet morning. Only one car on the racks. Everett was tightening bolts. Four other guys were sitting around drinking strawberry sodas and digging dirty fingers into a large bag of chocolate chip cookies.

Tyrell reached in for one. "Breakfast."

"Rodeo man," Wallace said to Danny. "You come to watch big men work on cars today?"

Danny grinned. "Looks like you're working on a bag of cookies."

Spike, the silver-toothed ex–auto thief, said, "Maybe we should send you out to spread some nails on the highway, work up some business."

"That would do it."

Danny went into the office to say hi to Ann, who was reading behind the counter.

"Good book?"

Ann held it up. *Lonesome Dove*. "Really good."

"You got to Blue Duck yet?"

"Blue Duck?"

"Best part in that book."

"*You've* read this? How old are you? Ten?"

Danny jumped up and sat on the counter. "Tyrell read it, too." He waggled his eyebrows.

"You twit," Ann said. "What'd you do to your elbow?"

Danny turned his arm over and rubbed the bruise he'd gotten in the cave with Banjo. "A tumble, s'all."

Ann eyed him.

He slipped off the counter and flopped down on a chair in the waiting area. He picked up a year-old copy of *People* magazine, then put it back down.

Ann watched him. "Tell me," she said. "You know I won't let it go."

Danny picked up the magazine again. "Banjo's missing," he mumbled. "He got . . . lost, or something."

Ann laughed. "Or something? Really? Just tell me what happened, Danny Mack."

Danny took a breath. "Actually . . . he got shot."

Ann gaped at him. "Oh, Danny . . ."

He told her all that had happened, then tossed the magazine onto the table and put his head in his hands. "We went back to look for him . . . but he was gone. . . . The sheriff wanted to take him away. He said I might never see him again."

"Couldn't you have found him a home?"

"We tried—me, Tyrell, my friends. We only had two days. No one would take him because we'd have to tell them he went after livestock, even though I know he'd never do that. But Mr. Brodie . . ."

Ann came out from around the counter and knelt in front of him. "I'm so sorry, Danny."

"I don't want to talk about it."

"Okay." She put a hand on his arm.

Outside, a shiny black BMW drove up, and Ann headed back around the counter. "Banjo will show up somewhere. Miracles happen."

The BMW guy came in, and Danny went back to the service bays.

Spike drove the guy's car in and racked it.

Danny helped him remove four good Pirellis from the shiny chrome rims. The guy wanted new Michelins. He said Schwab could keep the Pirellis. He had no use for them.

"You still miss Grouch?" Danny asked as they worked.

Spike stopped and rubbed his forehead with the back of his wrist. "Yeah, I do, but he's better off where he is now. He was pretty sick."

"Was he a good dog?"

Spike nodded. "Big, dumb, and always happy to see me when I came home." Spike rolled the four new Michelins over. "There's this stagnant pond out behind my house. Smells like a swamp. Grouch used to drink from it. I chased him away a thousand times." Spike shook his head. "He got sick. He was old and couldn't bounce back."

Spike set the Pirellis off to the side. "By the way, sorry I couldn't take your dog, Danny. Tyrell told me. My wife . . . you know, losing Grouch . . . that hit her hard."

"Yeah."

Spike said, "I think I'll put these Pirellis on my truck." He winked and went into the office to do the paperwork.

Danny sat on a stack of tires, rubbing grime off his hands with a red rag. Spike came back and eased down next to him. "Look at all this filth around my fingernails."

Danny snickered. "What do you expect? Look where you work."

Spike took a small pocket knife and dug under his thumbnail. "I've had grimy hands since I was two years old. What does that say about me, huh?"

"That you're a grease monkey?"

Spike laughed. "And proud of it. So tell me about Banjo."

Danny turned away. "I heard you're quitting."

Spike brightened. "You ever heard of Mammoth Lakes?"

"No."

"It's a ski resort down in California. My cousin offered me a job as a cook."

"With those hands?"

Spike checked them over. "I guess I could get them sandblasted. I'm a good cook, though. Now stop stalling and you tell me about your dog."

Danny frowned. "You ever feel like you didn't have the brains God gave a rock?"

"Every day, kid, every day."

"And then one day you do something and wish you hadn't, and there's no way you can undo it?"

"Been there."

Spike waited, a slight smile under narrowed eyes.

"I made a bad mistake, Spike."

"Join the crowd. We all do, at one time or another. But hopefully we learn from them. Now tell me what you did you couldn't take back."

Danny looked out the wide bay door at the sunny day.

"I'm not leaving you alone until you come up with a believable story," Spike said. "And I can smell a fake a mile away."

Danny told him everything.

In the end, Spike said, "You're right. That's a bad mistake. But I made a bad mistake, too . . . worse than yours."

Danny looked up. "Worse?"

"That stagnant pond that made my dog sick? I didn't fence it off."

29

That same evening at Meg's house, a huge pot of steaming chili sat on the kitchen table next to a pan of fresh-baked cornbread.

They ate in silence for a solid five minutes.

Without looking up, Mr. Harris finally said, "What are we going to do with the dog? It's been two days now." He was casual, the way he'd ask someone to pass him the salt.

Meg glanced at her mom. She knew Mom thought they already had too many animals around their place.

"Hey, Dad," Jeremy said. "Can I get a motorcycle?"

Jacob choked on a laugh.

"Nope," Mom said without looking at Jeremy.

"What about Banjo?" Meg blurted.

"Well," Mom said. "If he's lost, somebody will be looking for him. If he was abandoned, they won't. We'll give it two weeks. See if anyone puts up a sign. The dog needs to heal, anyway. We should take him to the vet, too. Maybe tomorrow."

Meg wondered what could happen in two weeks. And what if she had to give him up? That dog needed her.

"If I had a motorcycle," Jeremy went on, "I could get myself to school and you wouldn't have to drive me."

"Jeremy," Mr. Harris said. "You're too young. You need a license, just like for a car."

Jacob stared at the table. "I can't believe somebody just went and dumped it. You don't just throw your dog away."

"We don't know what happened," Mom said.

Jacob reached across the table and touched Meg's hand. "If anyone did, I say we peg him down over a red-ant hole."

Meg smiled. "I'm in," she said.

And Jeremy? She grinned at how he was pigging out across from her.

"What?" he said.

"Just watching you eat."

"Well, don't."

Jacob winked at her.

"Maybe the vet will know something about a lost dog," Mom said. "If not, we'll tack up some posters. If you make one tonight, we can make copies in the morning."

"Sure."

Mom rubbed soothing circles on Meg's back with her fingertips. "Don't worry, honey. We'll find his home."

Meg nodded, barely. She felt the same as Jacob. If somebody dumped Banjo, then he should be thrown into a nest of rattlesnakes. She wasn't so sure she wanted to find his home.

30

Tyrell had to work late, so one of the guys at Les Schwab gave Danny a ride home. Dad rolled in around six.

A while later, Danny sat cross-legged on the floor in the living room reading an article in *Western Horseman*. He'd been staring at the same paragraph for ten minutes.

Dad was reading *The Week* magazine, his feet up on the wood-slab coffee table, when someone knocked on the door. He started to get up.

"I'll get it," Danny said.

His breath caught when he opened the door.

"Evenin'," Mr. Brodie said, removing his hat. A black-and-white miniature Banjo puppy was tucked into his left arm.

Dad put the magazine down and stood. "Come on in, Harmon. Have a seat."

"Thank you, but I only got a minute."

Mr. Brodie tucked his hat under his arm and stroked the pup's head. "Been feelin' bad about your dog, Danny. Your dad told me you done it yourself." He shook his head, looking at the pup. "I had to shoot a dog once. Hardest thing I ever done in my life, even to this day. She just got too old."

Danny thought, So you came over here with a dog that looks like Banjo to rub it in?

"Anyways," Mr. Brodie went on. "Here. It's yours."

Danny gaped at him. "You're . . . you're *giving* me this puppy?"

Mr. Brodie held the puppy out. Danny couldn't help but take it. Its fur was soft and warm. Holding it in his hands made every dark thought about Mr. Brodie vanish.

"Border collie pup," Mr. Brodie said. "My Starleen had a litter of six. Good working dogs, especially the females. Know how to be around and protect livestock. This one's just over three months. She'll be a good dog for you."

Danny looked up at Mr. Brodie. Was this a joke?

"Weighs about as much as a ant, don't she?"

Dad peered over Danny's shoulder. "You didn't have to do this, Harmon."

"No. But like I said, I had to shoot a dog once myself." He looked at the floor. "Still think it had to be done, but . . . that don't make it a easy thing to do."

He buried his hand in his pocket. With his hat in his other hand he pointed to the pup. "She ain't completely housebroke yet, so put down some newspapers."

Danny fumbled for something to say. "Uh . . . thank you, sir. . . . She's a nice pup."

"Well," Mr. Brodie said. "Guess I'll go on home." He put his hat on and touched it with his fingers. "Danny. Ray."

"Stop by anytime, Harmon," Dad said.

Mr. Brodie ran a finger under the pup's chin, then nodded to Danny and left.

Dad scratched the puppy's head. "Better get some old papers and a bowl of water."

"Why'd he do this, Dad?"

"He's not a bad guy, Danny."

Danny looked at the puppy. "No . . . but—"

Dad put a hand on Danny's shoulder. "Banjo's gone, Danny. It's time to move on."

Danny opened his mouth to speak, but nothing came out.

31

After Mr. Brodie left, Danny squatted and let the pup explore. She moved pretty well on her young legs.

"What are you going to call her?"

"Let me think on that."

Danny got a slice of rope from his room. "How about a little tug-of-war, girl?"

His game with Banjo.

The puppy took hold and pulled, Danny remembering how Banjo loved tug-of-war. He hoped some kind person found him and took him home.

After a few minutes of playing with the puppy, Danny went out to the barn and cut up some old planks. He used them to block off a corner in the kitchen and filled the space inside with newspapers.

"Your own corral. When you get to where you piddle outside, I'll take this thing down. We got a deal?"

The pup walked lightly over the paper.

"You'll get used to it."

"Cute little thing," Dad said.

"Still can't believe Mr. Brodie brought it over."

"He did that for you, Danny."

Danny nodded.

"Well, I guess I'll head to bed. Thought of a name yet?"

"Yeah . . . Ruby."

"I like it."

Danny picked her up and held her nose to nose. She licked his face, a dog kiss.

"Hello, Ruby."

Danny set her back in the kitchen corral and looked at her. *This should feel better than it does.*

Not too much later, Tyrell came home. "Where'd you get the pup?" he asked, unbuttoning his grease-stained shirt.

"Mr. Brodie gave her to me."

Tyrell grinned. "You're kidding."

"Came over tonight. He said he felt bad about Banjo."

Tyrell stood watching Ruby in her corral. "He must have felt real bad, because that's a real nice border collie."

"Her name is Ruby."

Tyrell crouched down to pet her, then looked back up at Danny. "You think the Brodie boys know their dad gave you this pup?"

"Sure hope so."

Tyrell grinned.

32

At one o'clock in the morning, Danny woke to high-pitched cries coming from the kitchen. He got up, went out, and without turning the light on, stepped into Ruby's pen.

"Kind of lonely out here?"

He picked her up and nestled her in his lap. She licked his fingers and curled into a ball. Danny thought about taking her back to his room, but no, she might piddle.

"This will be the hardest night," Danny said. "I promise you'll get used to it."

He leaned back against the refrigerator. Banjo had whined a bit, too, when Danny first got him. He was bigger, but he still got lonesome.

"You lonesome, Ruby?"

Danny grabbed the tug-of-war rope from Ruby's corral and whipped it across the kitchen. He laid his head back on the refrigerator and closed his eyes.

I'm sorry, Banjo. I'm so, so sorry.

Eventually Ruby fell asleep and Danny set her down. He went to his room and put on his jeans, boots, and T-shirt.

Outside, a banana moon cast just enough light to make shadows in the yard. The night air was warm.

Danny headed into the barn. Tyrell had a set of weights and a boxer's heavy bag over in one corner that he slammed and hammered to build his strength and endurance.

Danny took off his T-shirt and put on a pair of boxing gloves. For a moment, he stood hugging the bag, listening to the rustling sound of some rodent in the barn.

He pushed the bag away, and when it swung back he laid into it.

Whack!

Whack!

Whack!

The bag swung out and came back, and Danny danced around it and poured his power into it.

Whack!

Whack-whack!

It felt good, especially when he hit it solid and the impact shot back through his arm to the muscles in his shoulders and his back.

Whomp! Whomp! Whomp-whomp!

Soon sweat stained the top of his jeans, and his bare chest and arms glistened. He bobbed in and out and around, raising dust around his boots, pummeling the bag.

For *Banjo!*

For *Banjo!*

For *Banjo!*

After ten minutes nonstop, he let the bag swing into him, grabbed and hugged it against his heaving, sweating chest.

Then he went at it again.

In a while he became aware of Dad leaning on the wall. That made him hit harder. His swelling fists inside the gloves were hot and sore.

The next time he looked, Dad was gone.

Enough . . . enough.

As he pulled the gloves off and hung them on the peg, a sense of peace fell over him. He was so tired nothing seemed to matter.

Under the open sky outside the barn, a star streaked across the night and vanished. All in all, that's about as long as his life would be. Then he'd be gone.

Not a whole lot of time to make things right.

He wiped the sweat and dirt from his face with his T-shirt, then took a deep breath and went inside.

Dad was sitting at the kitchen table with a cup of coffee and his magazine. Without looking up, he said, "Feel better?"

"I do."

Dad nodded.

Danny looked at him, drinking coffee in the dead of night because he cared about his lying, cruel, mean-spirited, mixed-up son.

"Well . . . g'night," Danny said, turning to leave.

Dad stood and took his cup to the sink. "Praise be. I was starting to think I might need another cup."

. . .

Danny sat on his bed. He had to make things right.

33

That same morning, Meg woke just before dawn.

She dressed fast, brushed her teeth, threw water on her face, and dried off. She hadn't slept well, worrying Banjo might just give up on living.

She ran outside.

Banjo wasn't in the barn.

She found him sitting in the pasture looking at the horses, his back to her.

The horses were bunched in the far corner, their heads turned toward him, not paying him much mind.

He hadn't given up, he'd *moved*!

"Thank you," Meg whispered.

She picked her way out into the dewy pasture. "Banjo," she said softly.

Banjo turned to look back. He woofed. One heavenly dog word that stopped Meg. It was the first sound he'd made since she'd found him.

She knelt in the wet grass, hoping he'd come to her.

But he sank down and put his head between his paws.

Meg stood and walked over to him. "You don't have a whole lot to say to people, do you?"

Banjo raised his head.

"You hungry, buddy? Thirsty?"

He woofed again.

Meg grinned. "Don't go anywhere. I'll be right back."

The house was quiet, but Meg could hear the shower running.

Wouldn't a hungry dog eat just about anything? She grabbed a large can of pork and beans and emptied it into an aluminum mixing bowl. Jeremy would kill her if he saw her feeding Banjo from his favorite popcorn bowl. Too bad.

Banjo stood when she put the bowl in front of him. Meg watched as he wiped the bowl clean, pushing it around in the grass with his nose until Meg finally took it away. She hoped feeding him beans wasn't a mistake. Too late for that!

She took the bowl to the water trough, rinsed it, and filled it halfway.

Banjo lapped up every drop.

"Good boy," Meg said. "Good, good, good."

She filled it again.

• • •

At nine-thirty, Meg and Mom urged Banjo into the Jeep. He circled around on the back seat and settled.

"He's done this before," Mom said.

As they drove, Meg said, "This morning he was out watching the horses. I think he was a ranch dog."

"That would be a good bet."

"So why would someone dump a good ranch dog?"

"Maybe he ran off."

"Seriously, Mom."

"Okay. Not likely."

"But what if it's true that he was abandoned? And what if no one claims him?"

Mom reached over and took Meg's hand. "Then we'll find him a home."

"Or maybe . . . keep him?"

"Why'd I know you'd ask that?"

34

Danny woke tired.

Thoughts of Banjo and slamming the heavy bag in the middle of the night had messed with his sleep. Still, he had chores.

Ruby followed him everywhere he went.

"Right off, Ruby, you got to learn something important about livestock," Danny said, carrying a bucket of feed out to the horses. "Rules number one, two, and three are you don't bark at them and you don't chase them. If you're with me, you can herd them. But you *never* chase 'em. Get that down before you think on rules number four, five, and six, which are, you don't chase livestock. Got it?"

Ruby stumbled through the pasture and past the steers, which were all bunched up and bug-eyed, especially the one Ricky called crazy. That one had her head down and was staring at them.

Ruby kept clear.

"Smart girl. Those critters would worry me, too, if I was your size."

He chuckled, thinking of how Ricky wanted to ride their crazy steer. The steer was just curious and maybe a bit wild. Seeing it throw Ricky for a loop would be a sight to see.

"Watch this, Ruby." Danny shook the bucket of feed. "The horses can hear food a mile away."

In less than a minute all four of them came trotting up from the gully. "What'd I tell you?"

The closer the horses came, the closer Ruby got to Danny, until she stood peeking between his boots.

Danny poured the feed and vitamins into four metal pans that were scattered in the grass. Pete, Mandingo, Half-Asleep, and Angelina nosed down to eat. "Y'all, meet Ruby," Danny said. "Not quite the size of Banjo, but . . ."

Just saying Banjo's name burned his throat.

Then a thought popped up. What if someone had found him and put up a lost-dog sign? Like in a grocery store or on a pole? Or they put an ad in the paper? And what if Dad or Mr. Brodie *saw* it?

Why hadn't he thought of that?

Danny picked Ruby up and ran back to the house.

The latest *Bend Bulletin* was on the floor under Ruby's sleeping towel. Danny knelt and tore through the pages. When Ruby walked on them, Danny had to push her away.

"Listen. This is important. I have to find . . . your big brother."

Ruby yawned.

Danny picked her up, held her close. "Someday I'll tell you all about it. Maybe."

He checked the lost-and-found animal notices.

"What you doing down there, little man?" Tyrell stepped over the barricade and squatted next to him.

"Looking for lost-dog notices."

"Find any?"

"Not yet."

"And what would you do if you did? You couldn't bring him here."

"I know, but if there's an ad, Dad or Mr. Brodie could see it."

Tyrell winced. "Right."

Danny flipped the pages.

"Shouldn't you be out there practicing for the rodeo?"

"Yeah, but I can't stop thinking about Banjo. I'll be lucky if I can rope a fence post. This is driving me *crazy*."

"Yeah." Tyrell took a deep breath. "I feel bad, too."

Danny looked up. "It was dumb."

Tyrell nodded. "I'm leaving for work in ten. Want to bring Ruby and come along?"

Danny crumpled the paper and threw it at the refrigerator. "Let's go."

Just then the phone rang. Tyrell grabbed it. "Macks' place."

He turned to Danny and mouthed, *It's Mom.*

Danny shook his head and ran outside.

35

The vet took her time checking Banjo over.

"No internal injuries that I can tell," Dr. Clarke said. "Just the surface wound, which seems to be taking care of itself. Where'd you find this dog?"

"Out near Camp Sherman," Meg said. "In the woods."

"Have you gotten any calls about a lost dog, Doctor?" Mom asked.

Dr. Clarke shook her head. "What would you like me to do? Don't know about his shots or anything, but otherwise he's fine. Seems a little depressed, maybe."

Meg glanced at Mom, who was chewing on her thumbnail.

Dr. Clarke lifted the tag. "Is this all there was? Banjo?"

"That's all he had on him."

"Maybe he's chipped."

"Chipped?"

"It's an ID tag on a tiny microchip that's injected just under the skin, usually between the shoulder blades. Let's see if he has one. Hang on. I'll be right back."

Mom ran her hand through Meg's hair. "You like Banjo, don't you?"

"I really do."

"He needs love, sweetie, and you're about the best person I can think of to give it to him."

Meg leaned into her shoulder.

Banjo lay on the table on his stomach, head up, panting lightly. He wasn't afraid of being there, which told Meg he'd been to a vet before. So why would someone who cared enough to take his dog to the vet abandon it? Maybe he wasn't dumped, and somehow got lost.

Dr. Clarke returned with a scanner. She flattened the fur on Banjo's back and ran the scanner over it.

"Bingo."

36

Less than a quarter mile from Dr. Clarke's veterinary clinic, Danny and Tyrell walked into the service bays at Tyrell's job, Danny carrying Ruby like a football.

"Hey, Spike," Danny said.

Spike grinned. "Is that fur ball real or stuffed?"

"Meet Ruby," Danny said. "She's mean, so keep your greasy fingers to yourself."

"That ain't a dog," Spike said, taking Ruby from him. "It's a flea off of one."

Everett called out, "Is that a border collie?"

Danny nodded. "Purebred."

The rest of the guys came over and took turns holding the pup, whispering to her, cooing, and Ruby licked their blackened fingers and smiling faces.

"Here," Danny said, taking Ruby back. "I want to show Ann."

Ann flew around the counter. "A puppy! What's its name?"

"Ruby."

"I *love* that name! You're not going to make her stay in Tyrell's truck, are you?"

"Nope. I'll show you."

Danny took the pup out to the service bay and turned a

big truck tire on its side. He tossed in some paper and clean rags and set Ruby on top of them. "The Goodyear Hotel."

"She needs water," Ann said.

"I'll get it," Danny said. "Hey, listen. My dad and I are entered in the Madras rodeo this Saturday. How'd you like to come see us rope?"

"I'd like that, Danny, really. But I'm not so much into—"

"Come on, it's gonna be great. You'll like it."

She peeked around him toward the service bays. "Is Tyrell going?"

"Yep."

"Does he compete, too?"

"Nope. But he helps with the horses and checks out the girls."

"Figures."

"We'll pick you up at seven. And wear a hat. It'll be hot."

Ann smiled and hooked her arm under his. "Can't wait, cowboy."

37

The name Dr. Clarke got from the microchip database was Steven Diaz of Portland, Oregon. But when they called his number, it was disconnected.

Dr. Clarke suggested that Meg place an ad in *The Oregonian* and call every Steven Diaz she could find in the Portland phone directory.

"He should have called and updated his file," she said. "Sometimes people forget the most important things."

Back home, Meg sat in the kitchen with her laptop, went online, and called the five "Steven Diaz" numbers she found.

Zero.

No one knew anything about a dog named Banjo.

Then she called everyone with the last name of Diaz.

Still nothing.

She crossed her arms on the table and laid her head down.

"What's up, squirt?" Jacob grabbed a chair, turned it around, and straddled it. "Something about the dog?"

Meg sat up and rubbed her face. "Now I know what 'needle in a haystack' means." She told him about the vet, the chip, and all the people she'd called.

Jacob smiled. "Back to Google. Let's try Beaverton."

One Steven Diaz listing. Meg called it. Nothing.

"Maybe he moved. Let's go across the river and try Vancouver."

One popped up.

Meg punched in the number. "Uh . . . is this Mr. Steven Diaz?"

"Yeah. Who's this?"

"Um . . . my name is Meg Harris. I live in Sisters, in central Oregon."

"Ah, Sisters. Been through there a thousand times. What can I do for you?"

"I think I found your dog . . . I mean he was lost, and hurt . . . I found him when I was out riding—"

"Wait, wait, hold on. I don't have a dog. You sure you got the right number?"

"Well, I got the name Steven Diaz from a dog ID on a microchip. His name is Banjo."

"Yeah, yeah, yeah . . . Banjo . . . I found that dog out on the road."

Meg turned to Jacob and gave him a smile and a thumbs-up.

Steven Diaz went on. "He wasn't more than a pup. Got nicked by a car, so I took him home to heal, then gave him to another trucker who had a small ranch out near Redmond. But that was a while back. Where's the dog now?"

"Here with me. In Sisters. We just took him to the vet."

"Is he hurt?"

"He was. But he'll be okay."

"What'd you say your name was?"

"Meg Harris."

"Hang on, Meg. I'll be right back." The phone clanked down. Meg could hear drawers opening and closing.

"I must have lost the guy's number when we moved," he said, picking up the phone. "The dog was for his son. Nice kid. I met him with his dad once, over in Bend."

"He lives in Redmond?"

"Near Redmond. I wonder how he lost the dog."

"We don't know."

"Banjo's the sweetest, gentlest animal in the history of four-legged creatures."

"I like his name," Meg said.

Steven Diaz chuckled. "I named him in honor of Earl Scruggs, the best banjo player of his time. So listen, Meg. Give me your number, and I'll call you if I find that boy's information."

She gave him her number. "What's the boy's name, Mr. Diaz?"

"His dad's name is Ray. Don't know the boy's. Can't recall the last name, either. But it'll come to me."

After she hung up she looked at Jacob. "Banjo belongs to a boy in Redmond. His dad's name is Ray. That's all I got."

"Good enough to start asking questions."

38

WEDNESDAY

The next morning Meg and Jacob made a lost-dog sign and twenty copies. They drove east and nailed them up, beginning over in Redmond and ending up back in Sisters. Maybe the mystery boy would see one.

"Don't hope for too much from this, Meg," Jacob said.

"Why not?"

"If this kid lost his dog, wouldn't he be the one putting up the flyers?"

39

Danny called the animal shelter and checked the paper.

Nothing new.

Banjo just *vanished*.

He found Tyrell in his room, getting ready to go to Bend on his day off. "You have to drive me back to Camp Sherman, just one last time."

Tyrell shook his head. "It's been five days. He's long gone. You got to let this go."

"I can't. I have to know if someone found him."

"Then what?"

"I don't know."

"This is nuts."

But Tyrell took him to Camp Sherman anyway. One last time.

If anyone knew anything, it would be at the store.

Zero. Zip. No found dogs.

They drove back through Sisters slowly, looking for signs tacked to telephone poles. They checked Ray's Grocery at the far end of town, then worked their way east.

They read every sign they came across.

Nothing about a dog.

They stopped at stores and asked. Came up empty.

Maybe Banjo was dead. Maybe coyotes got him. Or he hooked up with a pack of feral dogs.

"Got to get you home," Tyrell said.

But just outside of Sisters, they saw a girl tacking a piece of paper to a fence post. Then she jumped into a Jeep that took off toward town.

The guy at the wheel glanced at them as he passed.

"He look familiar?" Tyrell said.

"No, but pull over. Let's see what they put up."

Danny jumped out and read it.

```
Medium sized black and white dog
      found near Camp Sherman.
         Tag says "Banjo."
```

There was a name, Meg Harris.

And a phone number.

Danny's heart slammed in his chest. Banjo was *alive*! He wanted to race after the Jeep, catch up and tell them, *That's my dog! Where is he? Can I see him? Can I take him home?*

He ripped the sign off the post and jammed it into his pocket.

40

When Meg and Jacob got home from tacking up the lost-dog signs, they found a note taped to the fridge in the kitchen.

Meg—there's a message for you on the answering machine.

Meg hit the play button.

"Meg, this is Steven Diaz in Vancouver. It finally came to me. The kid's name is Danny Mack. I hope that helps. Let me know how this plays out, will you? You have my number. Thanks."

"I know that name," Jacob said. "Danny Mack."

"You *know* him?"

Jacob squinted, thinking. "If it's the same guy . . . there's this rodeo kid named Danny Mack, kind of a genius roper I read about in the paper. I think he's about thirteen, fourteen. Something like that."

"The one I'm looking for lives near Redmond."

Jacob shrugged. "Call him. Or better, there's an open rodeo over in Madras this weekend. I'd bet nags to purebreds he'll be in it. He's kind of a crowd-pleaser, because he's a kid and so good. You can ask him face to face."

Meg's stomach turned, as if she were too close to finding

something she didn't want to find. She realized how attached she'd become to Banjo.

And what if this kid really *had* abandoned him? Would he get angry at her for bringing Banjo back? Would he deny the dog was his? Or would he fake how glad he was to have found Banjo, then take him away and do it all over again?

Meg jumped when the phone rang.

Jacob picked it up. "Hey, Dex, what's up?"

Meg started to leave.

Jacob grabbed her arm. "Dex wants to talk to you."

She grabbed the phone. "What?" she said.

"Is that any way to greet a friend?"

"Friend? You shot at my *cat*."

"Yeah, well, I wanted to apologize for that."

"Who is this? Not the Dex I know, that's for sure."

Dex laughed. "You're right. But the other Dex is truly sorry and promises he won't do it again."

"Good." Meg hung up.

41

When Danny got home he gave Ruby some water, let her out, and pulled the lost-dog sign from his pocket. *What do I do?*

"Be back later," Tyrell said. He nodded to the lost-dog sign. "Good luck with that."

"Hey . . . thanks for taking me today."

"Where should I send the bill?"

Danny grunted. "Send it to Billy Brodie."

He picked up the phone to call Meg Harris.

Then put it down.

What would he say? And did he want to take such a risk? If he got Banjo back, then what? Wouldn't it be better to just let it be?

The phone rang.

Danny stared at it. What if it was Mr. Brodie? What if he'd been up to Sisters and had seen one of the girl's signs?

What if, what if, what if?

He let it go to voice mail.

Then listened to it.

"Ray, it's Harmon. Would you give me a call when you get in? I'd appreciate it."

Danny's gut felt like a volcano. What did he want?

Maybe it wasn't about Banjo.

And maybe it was.

He had to take those signs down. *Today!*

Ruby started yapping outside.

Danny jammed the sign into his pocket and looked out the window. No Ruby.

He went out. Sounded like she was somewhere behind the barn. When he spotted her, he shouted, "Ruby! Get away from there!"

She'd raised a rattlesnake.

"Ruby! Come here!"

Danny ran up, then slowed, not wanting to trigger the snake. Ruby backed off, still yapping.

The rattler was standing tall in the weeds, ready to strike.

Danny grabbed Ruby and stumbled back, hands trembling. Snakes didn't scare him, but the thought of losing Ruby did. He tossed a rock at the rattler to chase it away before it slithered into the barn.

Danny put Ruby in the house and shut the door tight. He grabbed his bike and raced out to the road. If Mr. Brodie came over, he didn't want to be there.

He headed to Sisters.

He'd take the signs down. All of them.

It was a long ride. He pumped until his thighs burned and still kept going.

"*Ahhh!*" he shouted into the stillness of the country road. If he didn't get his life back soon, his performance at the rodeo would be a disaster. And he'd take Dad down with him.

He was beat when he finally got to Sisters. He bought a

cold bottle of water, then scoured the town, trying not to look sneaky. He took down every "Banjo" sign he could find.

They were all over the place.

He rode up and down the two main streets, searching until he'd gotten them all.

Maybe.

42

The sky was turning purple black by the time he got home.

Tyrell was still gone. And Dad.

He took Ruby and headed out toward a high knoll where he could see the road coming up to the house. Along the way, he angled over to the ridge that looked down onto the Brodie place. What happened that night? Why would Banjo dig under the fence to chase sheep? What would cause him to do that when he never had before? Was there really a pack of wild dogs?

It didn't make sense.

Danny was about to head back over to the knoll when he kicked something in the grass. He bent to pick it up.

An empty beer bottle.

He raised it to his nose. It hadn't been out there long.

Beer? Who drank beer?

He looked around for more but didn't find any. He took the bottle back to the barn so one of the steers or horses wouldn't kick it and cut up its feet.

When he came back out, he saw Ruby running down to the trees where the horses were. He whistled for her to come back, but she kept on going. She'd be safe over there.

He strode over to the knoll, thinking he had to call Meg

Harris. If he didn't, she'd probably keep putting up signs, and sooner or later Mr. Brodie was bound to see one.

Danny looked back when he heard the growl of a truck.

Headlights coming up the drive.

Dad.

Danny whistled and waved, got a horn tap back.

The time had come. Something needed to change. He had to tell the truth about Banjo. If he didn't, and Dad found out from someone else, the whole mess would explode into something worse than it already was.

The lies end here.

Dad got out of the truck, reached in, got a paper bag, and headed to the knoll.

He scrambled up the rock and sat next to Danny.

In the west, a long thin layer of red cut under dark clouds on the horizon. The mountains silhouetted below looked like the edge of a saw.

Danny stalled, wanting a few more minutes of feeling good before blowing his dad's trust to shreds. "What's in the bag?"

"Take a look. It's for you."

Danny peeked in. "Yes!" He threw the bag aside and cradled the new Bushnell riflescope. It was heavy and smooth. "Perfect. Thanks!"

"Thought you should have one for the Winchester."

Danny pulled off the lens protectors and put the scope to his eye. "Wow," he said. "You can make out the lettering on the mailbox, even in this light."

"With that you'll see the hair on an elk's ear."

"Great, Dad, just great."

Dad nodded toward the gully. "I see she's getting the lay of the land."

Danny whistled, and Ruby looked up. "Come here, girl."

She bounded toward them, and Danny lifted her into his lap. "She almost shook hands with a rattler today, out behind the barn."

"You shoot it?"

"Chased it away."

He had to remember to check and see if the snake had come back, and if it had, chase it away again. Or else capture it and take it way out into the rocks. Shooting it would solve the problem, but Danny didn't want to kill it. They ate rodents and diggers.

Dad reached over and let Ruby lick his fingers. "Mr. Brodie's a stand-up guy, bringing you this pup."

Danny nodded.

"You out here thinking about Banjo again?"

Danny stroked Ruby's head. "It's like a nightmare I can't wake from."

"You've got to get over it, Danny. Things like this happen in the country."

Danny nodded.

They got up and walked toward the house. Dad put his arm around Danny's shoulder and tugged him close. "That all that's bothering you, son?"

Tell him.

"Dad I . . . I . . . just tired, is all."

"Turn in early. We've got a big weekend coming up. We need you rested with a clear mind. I hope you haven't let up on your practice."

He'd let up way more than he should have. But he had two days left to make up for it. "I've tossed a rope some, but I need to spend more time with Pete."

"I'm here most of the day tomorrow and Friday morning. We'll run some drills."

"Tyrell's got work, but maybe I can get Ricky to come over."

"If he can't, we'll make do."

Dad looked up at the night sky, now starting to speckle with stars. "What an evening."

The phone rang inside the house.

"I'll get it." Danny ran in.

"Hello? This is Danny."

"Your dad home? I'd like to talk with him."

Mr. Brodie.

43

It got hot early the next day.

By nine o'clock, Danny and Tyrell had worked up a sweat out in the pasture working on the stump. Dad had to make a run to town, but was always ready with something they could do around the place. "We're never going to get that stump out if we don't keep digging at it," he'd said.

Dynamite would work better, Danny thought.

He and Tyrell leaned on their picks, studying the stump. Almost four feet across. They'd done a fair amount of digging already, but not near enough to start rocking it out.

"Why doesn't Dad just get a backhoe to take this out?" Danny said.

"Money. Besides, he's got us."

"Right."

After twenty minutes of pummeling the ground around the stump, Danny looked up to see Ricky making his way over from the barn.

"You forgot your pick," Danny called.

"That's grunt work," Ricky said. "Anyway, I have a better idea than hacking at a stump."

"*Any* idea is a better idea than this," Tyrell said. "What is it?"

Ricky pulled a beat-up leather glove out of his rear pocket. "Today I ride your crazy bull."

Danny groaned. "It's a *steer,* not a bull."

"So? He acts like a bull."

Tyrell sank his pick into the stump. "I like it."

Danny grinned at Ricky. "I guess it would be fun to see that beast stomp your butt into the dirt."

Ricky smiled. "Now you're talking. Let's do it."

Danny saddled Pete, then cut the wild steer out of the bunch and, along with Tyrell and Ricky, hazed him into the working pen.

The steer lowered his head and hoofed the dirt. He looked mean with his ten-inch horns, but Danny knew he wasn't. He just had an attitude.

"Hoo-ee," Tyrell said, keeping clear of the steer. "He wants your hide, Ricky. You sure you want to do this?"

"Oh yeah." He pulled his bull-riding glove on. "Let's go get him."

Danny, on Pete, roped the steer and pulled him toward the roping chute. It wasn't a perfect situation. A real bull-riding chute opened to the side, not front. But this would do. Tyrell and Ricky pushed and shoved and snugged him up close to the front. Danny slid off Pete and stuck a board through the fencing to keep the steer from backing up.

Ricky climbed the fence and looked down on the steer. "Got a piece of rope we can tie around his belly? I need something to hang on to."

Danny got one from the barn, and Ricky and Tyrell

ran the rope around the steer's chest, just behind the front legs. They pulled it up tight. "That ought to do it," Tyrell said.

"Now, to get on this thing," Ricky said. "You two hold him tight. He's not going to like me on his back."

Danny and Tyrell each took one side of the steer to hold him in place. "How we going to get out of the way when we turn him loose?" Danny said, looking at Tyrell across the steer's back. "He could go out kicking."

"Climb over the fence after I get on," Ricky said. "Open the gate when I say."

Ricky got up on the fence and lowered himself down onto the steer's back.

The steer jumped forward, snorted, and tried to climb the gate.

Tyrell and Danny leaped out of the way but came back when the steer settled down. "Hurry up," Tyrell said.

The steer kicked and leaned into Danny, pushing him into the fence. Danny slapped its rump and the steer shifted toward Tyrell.

Ricky worked his gloved hand under the rope.

"Aren't you supposed to tie your hand down?" Danny asked.

"On a real bull, yeah. But for a little guy, this will do."

"Five hundred pounds isn't so little," Tyrell said.

Ricky raised his eyebrows. "That what he weighs?"

"Looks like it."

Danny shoved the steer. It was crowding him again. "Come on. He's gonna squash me."

"Okay," Ricky said. "Get the gate."

Danny climbed over the fence.

Tyrell got up on the top rung and sat with his feet on the steer, trying to hold him in place.

Ricky pulled his hat low and held tight. He nodded. "Go!"

Danny sprang the gate open.

Tyrell reached down and slapped the steer's rump. *"Haw!"*

He did it again. *"Hawww!"*

The steer just stood there.

Tyrell shoved it with his foot. "Git! Go!"

The steer turned to look at him.

When they realized the steer wasn't going anywhere, Danny and Tyrell cracked up. They staggered around, laughing at Ricky.

"Come on!" Ricky shouted. "Buck, you lazy beast!"

Nothing.

Danny pointed at Ricky on the parked steer. "That has got to be the funniest thing I've ever seen!"

"Dang," Ricky said.

He got off and, together with Tyrell, pushed the steer out of the chute. "Show's over. You can go home."

The steer walked out into the arena and looked back at them, the rope around his chest beginning to slip off.

"He's a wild one, all right," Danny said, still laughing.

The steer lowered its head and trotted over to the open gate. Danny watched it meander out into the pasture. For thirty minutes he hadn't thought a thing about what he'd done to Banjo.

It all came rushing back.

44

FRIDAY

On Friday, Danny and Dad brought two steers into the arena and took turns roping and running the chute. They practiced for three hours, and the whole time Danny worried about what Dad and Mr. Brodie had talked about on the phone. Dad hadn't said a word about that conversation.

But if he'd called about Banjo, Dad would have been all over it.

Wouldn't he?

Just after they'd sent the steers back out into the pasture, Mr. Brodie came dusting up the drive.

He parked, got out, and put on his hat. "Ray. Danny."

Dad and Mr. Brodie shook hands. "How's the family?" Dad said.

"Good, good. Boys like to work less and less, though. Must be the age."

Dad nodded.

"So—what I called about . . . ," Mr. Brodie said.

A wave of fear washed over Danny, his hands instantly sweating. *He saw the dog sign.*

Dad turned to Danny. "Go on and get the post-hole digger for Harmon, would you?"

Danny hesitated. *What?*

"You forget where it is?"

"Ah . . . no, no . . . I'll get it."

He headed to the toolshed and laid his head against the
door.

*I can't live like this. Tell Dad. Tell him as soon as Mr.
Brodie leaves.*

He took a deep breath, got the post-hole digger, and
brought it out.

"Keep it as long as you want," Dad said. "We won't need
it anytime soon."

"Appreciate it."

Mr. Brodie drove off.

Tell him!

"Dad, I . . ."

He stopped. He couldn't do it. Not before the rodeo. In
the arena, Dad had to trust him. Every second.

". . . I think I'll stay out here and rope the dummy for a
while."

Dad nodded and went into the house.

45

Meg woke and sprang up: *Rodeo day. Danny Mack.*

This was the day she would find him, this kid she didn't like.

In the kitchen, Dad was towering over a huge mess on the counter. He smiled. "Homemade pancakes. Want some?"

Meg looked at the box of Bisquick. "Homemade, huh?"

"Made them at home, didn't I?"

"Thanks, Dad, but I'm not hungry."

Jacob and Jeremy stumbled in and hunched over the table. Mr. Harris handed each of them a plate stacked with pancakes.

Meg managed one, then pushed her chair back. "Thanks for making breakfast, Dad. It was good."

"That all you're having?"

"I have to check on Banjo."

Jeremy grabbed her plate and scraped her leftovers onto his.

"Oink," she said.

Banjo was sitting out in the pasture watching the horses again. He stood when he saw her.

"Come, Banjo. Come here, boy."

He hesitated, then reluctantly came toward her, head down, tail brushing the grass. He stopped halfway and sat.

Meg sighed but was pleased that he'd at least done that much.

If Danny Mack showed one ounce of not caring for Banjo, she'd walk away, just like that.

"Meg?"

Mom tiptoed out into the dewy pasture in her sheepskin slippers with a plate of leftover pancakes. "I thought Banjo might like these."

Meg took one and held it up. "Look what I've got for you."

Banjo snatched it and ate it in two gulps. He looked up for more.

"Wow!" Meg said. "Who knew pancakes were the key?"

Mom pulled Meg close. "If we don't find who he belongs to, you can keep him."

"Really?"

"But you'll have to do all the extra work. This place is turning into a zoo."

"You know I will."

"Give him another pancake before his eyes bug out."

Meg gave him the last two, then knelt and rubbed his back, his pancake breath warm on her face.

"Mom . . . how can you tell if someone abandoned his dog? He sure wouldn't tell you."

"No."

"I guess Banjo's not lost at all, is he?"

"Listen," Mom said. "If it feels wrong to give Banjo back, we won't. But people should have a chance to have their say."

"His story better be good, then, because if it isn't, I'll have *my* say."

46

Tyrell and Danny left early that morning to pick Ann up. It was a clear and sunny high desert day, no wind to kick up dust. Perfect weather for rodeo competition. Danny was sorry Ricky had to miss it, but he had to go to Medford with his family. Danny grinned, thinking of him sitting in the chute on the stock-still steer.

After a few minutes of silence, Danny turned to Tyrell. "Want to hear something weird?"

"Tell me."

"Couple days ago I found an empty beer bottle up on the ridge. There was still some beer in it."

"Strange. How you suppose it got there?"

Danny looked at him.

Tyrell laughed. "Wasn't me, little brother."

"Then who?"

"Ghosts," Tyrell said.

Danny looked out the window, the country rolling by, gold and clean in the morning sun. Ghosts. Almost funny, because the mysterious beer bottle haunted him.

Danny closed his eyes and slept until they got to Ann's house.

. . .

"Thanks for inviting me," Ann said as she sat between them on the bench seat in Tyrell's truck. She elbowed Danny. "Nervous?"

"Me?"

"The rodeo."

He held out a hand. "Steady as a tire iron."

Of course he *was* nervous. If he ever wasn't, then that was when he should be. Nerves gave him a sharper edge.

"Don't you need a horse?" Ann asked.

Tyrell barked a laugh.

"Dad drove the horses over this morning," Danny said.

Warm air flowed in the window. Danny took a deep breath. "Love that country air."

"Smells like cow manure," Ann said.

"That's what I mean."

Ann laughed. "Cowboys."

"Tie-down roper, ma'am," Tyrell said. "That's what he is. Team roper, too."

Danny tapped the door with his hand. "I'm hoping to get a rodeo scholarship at Colorado State and compete in the college nationals."

Ann smiled. "I hope you do, too. . . . And don't you boys call me ma'am."

Tyrell turned to her. "Yes, miss."

She slugged him.

"Hey. That's my tire-changing arm."

Danny drifted off in a confusion of thoughts.

Banjo.

Meg Harris.

Dad.

Lies.

Stop! Focus!

He couldn't let Dad down in the arena. They were a team. If one of them couldn't concentrate, they'd both pay the price.

He'd call Meg right after the rodeo.

And he'd tell Dad the truth . . . tonight.

Looking at the landscape made him feel lighter; it filled him with something good, this place of outrageous skies, mountains, icy clean waters that flowed in creeks and streams and rivers. Dad called it "God's country."

Up ahead, trucks and cars were lined along the road, turning off toward the rodeo grounds. Danny clicked on country music radio to get into the spirit.

Ann leaned forward. "I love this!"

Tyrell tapped to the beat on the steering wheel as they turned in. When they parked, Danny jumped out and offered his hand to Ann.

"Thank you, Mr. Tie-Down Roper."

Danny touched his hat. "A pleasure, miss." He cracked up.

Danny wore a silver rodeo buckle, a blue snap-button shirt, and his black Resistol triple-X hat, pulled down to his ears, shading his face, almost hiding it. There wasn't anything else in the world as good as rodeo. Except maybe Ricky's mom's peach pie.

Ann hooked one arm through his and one through Tyrell's as they headed toward the arena. They walked along with women in tight jeans, some wearing wide-brimmed hats like Danny's, and guys in Wranglers with belts and big silver buckles.

"We need to find Dad," Danny said. "But first, let's get you a seat with the sun to your back 'fore they're all taken."

Tyrell ran ahead and picked out a spot, dead center.

As Ann sat down, Danny said, "See you in a bit. I got to get ready."

Tyrell touched Ann's shoulder. "Save my seat. I'll check in with Dad, then get us something to drink."

"Don't worry about me. Great people watching."

Danny and Tyrell headed down the stands.

47

Higher up, and a little to the right, Jacob leaned close to Meg. "See the guy down there in the blue shirt and black hat with that other guy showing the blonde where to sit? That's Danny Mack."

Meg watched them, eight or ten rows down. They were laughing. She couldn't see much of Danny's face because of his hat. But the girl was pretty.

"So there he is," Jeremy said. "You going to ask him about the dog?"

"Maybe."

Jeremy spat between his feet. "Dog dumper."

Mrs. Harris leaned over and glared at him. "No spitting."

"Sorry."

"He doesn't look like a dog dumper," Meg said.

Strangely, she hoped this boy wasn't the Danny Mack she was looking for. He looked nice.

Danny and the other guy made their way down the stands and headed toward the rough-stock pens.

Meg stood.

"Go get him," Jacob said.

"Yep." She started down, heading toward the chutes, where the contestants were.

It was a different world back there.

Men and boys barely out of high school milled around, brooding, thinking whatever they thought before going out to get stomped and broken.

She moved through them.

Who are you, Danny Mack?

48

Tyrell headed over to the concessions as Danny made his way past the stock pens to find Dad and get Pete warmed up.

The Brahma bulls were bug-eyed and kicking up dust. Danny stopped and looked them over, leaning on the metal rails along with the silent wranglers who'd be riding them. Some weren't much older than he was, but every one of them was iron tough. Some walked with slight limps. Some squatted down to peer through the fencing. Others leaned up against walls, unmoving. One looked about twelve.

Danny jumped back as a huge snorty bull came at him. Then it hopped up on another bull, raising a cloud of dust. He couldn't imagine getting up on a Brahma. Guys who did were made of something he wasn't.

He sensed someone watching him and turned to look.

A girl. Long blond hair, tied back. Light blue eyes, serious. He touched his hat.

49

Meg froze.

That's him, watching the bulls!

She took a step back. Her scalp prickled.

He looked to be about her age, and yet older at the same time. Middle school face, high school body.

He turned and looked at her.

Meg stopped breathing. Something inside made her stop.

Slowly Danny Mack reached up and touched the brim of his hat with his thumb and two fingers.

Meg backed away. Heat rushed to her face. She wanted to turn back and face him. But she was so embarrassed, caught looking at him.

She shoved her way through the crowd, back to the stands. This wasn't going the way she wanted it to.

Someone grabbed her arm. "Hey, slow down," Jacob said. "You running from something?"

"No . . . I'm not . . . I mean . . ."

"You talk to him?"

She shook her head. "I couldn't."

Jacob looked over her head at the stock pens. "Well, I sure can."

"No! Jacob, don't. Let me do this my way, okay?"

"All right. I'll stay out of it . . . for now."

"I can do this," Meg said. "I just need to think it through."

Jacob mussed her hair and headed over to the concessions.

Meg leaned against a metal rail.

I'll just go back and tell him I have his dog. What's so hard about that? It's not like I'm asking him for anything, or wanting something from him. I have a dog that might be his. That's all.

She started back toward the stock pens. *I'll say, Are you Danny Mack? And if he says he is, I'll say, Did you lose a dog? And if he says he did, then I'll say, Well seriously, how does somebody lose a dog?*

That's what she'd say.

But Danny Mack was gone.

50

Danny frowned. All he did was touch his hat, and the girl bolted. What was that about?

He removed his hat and checked it for dust, then put it back on. Did he know her? He didn't think so.

He walked back toward the arena, where she'd gone, but stopped short when he turned the corner. She was talking with some guy who towered over her.

Danny backed away.

He had to focus on what he was here to do, not follow some girl around. By now, Dad would be spitting nails.

But Dad just gave him a nod. "Nervous?"

"Yes."

"Good. Let's get these horses ready. Where's Tyrell?"

"Concessions. He'll be along."

Danny'd entered two events—individual tie-down first, and team roping later.

Pete stood relaxed as Danny gave him a quick brush down, saddled him, checked everything carefully, and swung aboard. He walked Pete around in back of the arena. They moved into a gentle trot and went right to loping to take the edge off both of them.

Danny came back, dismounted, and checked his gear once more. Everything was tied down tight.

"Ready?" Dad said.

Danny nodded.

Tyrell came back with three cold bottles of water and handed them around. They all took a drink.

Dad set his bottle down and reached out his arms. "Come here, boys."

As always before competition, they gathered in a huddle, arms around each other's shoulders as Dad spoke. "We all know our jobs and we do them well, but that doesn't mean there's no danger in a rodeo arena. Danny, you stay focused, and don't think too much. Let your training carry you through. And let us all be reminded to treat the animals and ourselves with respect, and let the miracle which created us all always keep us safe. We good?"

"Good!"

They broke apart.

Danny grabbed his rope and piggin' string and got back on Pete.

When his time came, he walked Pete over to the three-sided box next to the calf chute. He held his coiled rope in his left hand and shook out a loop with his right. He tucked the tail end of the piggin' string under his belt and held the looped end in his teeth. He turned his head to the side and pulled the string up to make sure he had enough slack so it wouldn't get jerked out while he was in the ring.

He backed Pete into the box.

The girl.

Who was she? Why'd she been looking at him? And why'd she run off?

Don't think about her! Only about this!

It was just him and Pete getting out of that box and onto the calf. The only thing that existed in the world was the calf, eyes on the calf.

Danny backed Pete crossways to the rear corner so both he and Pete could see the chute.

The girl popped back.

No!

You're on Pete.

You're in the box.

Watch your calf.

He leaned forward, boots braced in the stirrups.

In a minute it would be over.

When the calf faced forward, Danny nodded to the gateman.

The gate flew open.

The calf burst out of the chute.

When the rope barrier that held Danny back snapped, Pete leaped forward, knowing just where to go, what to do, how close to follow. Danny leaned into the run, felt the rush of speed, watching the calf's back, the head, the horns. He forgot the crowd, the arena, the burning sun.

There was Pete, the calf, and his rope.

He swung once, then again. On the third swing he let the loop fly. It sailed out and settled around the calf's head perfectly.

Pete pulled up and dug in.

Danny yanked the slack and pitched it up, then tagged Pete to tell him he'd be dismounting. In the same motion, he dismounted on the right, in position to grab and lift the calf with his stronger arm, keeping low, hitting the ground, running.

With his left hand on the rope, he ran down the line toward the calf. Pete pulled back, holding the rope taut. When Danny reached the calf, he grabbed its neck with his left hand where the rope was. He dug his left knee into the calf's shoulder, then reached over with his right hand and gripped its flank. With a massive burst of strength, he flipped the calf clean on its side, lifting then dropping it so fast and hard the calf's hooves came off the ground. If they didn't, he'd suffer a ten-second penalty.

Calf down, Danny grabbed its two back legs and one front leg, took the piggin' string from his teeth, and whipped it around the feet, three wraps and a half-hitch hooey.

Done!

He stood and raised his hands, time!

He walked back to Pete, mounted, and moved him forward, taking the tension off the rope.

The field flagger rode up to check the tie. It had to hold for six seconds.

It did.

Two wranglers ran out and untied the calf. It got to its knees, stood, and trotted out a gate at the far end of the arena, no worse for the wear.

Danny coiled his rope and laid it over his saddle horn.

One of the wranglers gave him his piggin' string back. "Nice job, kid."

Danny nodded, then grinned as his time came over the loud speaker.

"Ten point two seconds. Good enough to put the young man from Redmond in second place. Give Danny Mack a big hand, folks. He's only thirteen years old. You're gonna hear a whole lot about this homegrown cowboy in the years to come."

Danny finally became aware of the crowd. He looked up, raised his hat, put it back on. Ann and Tyrell were standing and waving at him, yelling. He looked for the girl but saw only colors and blurs.

Six cowgirls raced in on horseback with colorful flags to circle the arena, waving and smiling at the crowd.

Danny rode out slowly.

I'll call Meg Harris tonight.

51

Meg watched Danny's event from a seat in the fourth row, just down from the blond girl. Out there roping, he'd surprised her. What he'd done was a thing of beauty.

Something wasn't right.

A boy who was that good with a horse could never abandon a dog. There was more to this than she understood. Time to figure it out.

Just as she stood to go looking for him, the blond girl passed down the aisle.

Meg froze.

The girl smiled at her and continued down the stairs.

Without thinking, Meg called, "Wait a minute."

The girl turned, her smile changing to a look of curiosity.

When Meg got out to the aisle, the girl asked, "Do I know you?"

Meg shook her head. "No . . . but . . . you're with Danny Mack, right? The guy who just . . ."

The girl beamed. "Wasn't he *fantastic*?"

Meg nodded. "Yeah, he was good."

"Do you know Danny?"

"No, but . . ."

If Meg said she wanted to meet him, she'd sound like some cowboy groupie.

The young woman tipped her head to the side. "Want to walk with me? I'm thirsty."

"Sure."

"I work with Danny's brother at Les Schwab," Ann said. "Sometimes Danny comes in with him. He's a really nice kid, dedicated."

"He works at Les Schwab?"

"Not yet, but he's hoping to. What's your name?"

"Meg."

"I'm Ann."

They headed toward the concessions. The bronc riders were up now, but Meg didn't care if she missed seeing one of them get hammered.

"Danny's such a sweetheart," Ann said.

"He looks older than thirteen."

"Yeah, he's big for his age."

"Kind of like my brothers," Meg mumbled. "Well, anyway, I need to tell him that . . . I . . . think I found his dog."

Ann stopped and grabbed Meg's arm. "Banjo? You found *Banjo*?"

So it is *this Danny Mack.*

Meg nodded. "That was the name on the tag."

"My, my, my," Ann said. "You found Banjo. We are going to make that boy's day."

Ann hooked her arm through Meg's. "Let's go find the man. I want to see the look on his face when we tell him."

"Me too," Meg said.

52

Danny had the saddle off Pete and was currying him down. "You did good out there, bud," Danny whispered. "One more event, and you can go home and tell Angelina and Half-Asleep all about it."

Dad stood leaning against the horse trailer, watching Danny. "I think you could shave a couple tenths of a second off your time if you tie your hooey with two wraps 'stead of three."

"Maybe. But it might not hold."

"And maybe it would."

Danny nodded and was about to say he'd give it a try but was stopped cold by the sight of Ann coming his way . . . with the girl he'd caught staring at him.

Dad turned to see what he was looking at.

Ann smiled and waved. "Danny! You'll never believe this. This is Meg Harris, and she found Banjo!"

53

Dad stiffened and glared at Danny, eyes burning. Then he nodded to Meg and Ann. "Ladies." He touched his hat.

Ann smiled and introduced herself and Meg.

Meg shook his hand. "Nice to meet you, Mr. Mack."

"Please. Call me Ray."

Danny waited. His gut felt like lead, his face hot.

"Well," Dad said, without a glance at Danny, "if you all will excuse me, I think I'll pick up something to drink. It's hotter'n a burnt boot."

Danny winced and went back to brushing Pete.

Ann suddenly slapped her hand over her mouth. "Ohhh, Danny, you didn't tell him, did you? I'm so sorry."

"It's not your fault."

A moment of awkward silence.

Meg looked from one to the other.

Ann changed the mood. "You were fabulous out there, Danny. I had no idea you were that good. Why didn't you tell me?"

"What's to tell?"

Danny peeked at the girl, then away.

"Such modesty," Ann said. "Well, you were great."

"Nothing wrong with second place, I guess."

"I don't know how you picked up that calf and threw it on its side like that. Aren't they heavy?"

"Yeah, but you don't notice it when you're doing it."

Again, Danny glanced at Meg. Their eyes locked.

"Oh!" Ann said. "I'm so sorry. Meg, this is Danny Mack."

Danny gave her a hesitant nod.

"How'd you lose your dog?" Meg snapped.

Danny stopped brushing Pete. He stared at the ground. *Get a grip.*

"He had a tag on him that said Banjo," Meg added. "Black-and-white dog? Ring a bell?"

Danny stumbled for something to say. "You . . . you found Banjo? How . . . is he?"

Meg glared at him.

Danny saw that she knew he was playing dumb.

"How'd you lose him? Tell me that. I found him out near Camp Sherman. Don't you live, like, thirty miles away?"

How could he tell her the truth? She'd think he was a skunk. But if he continued to lie, she'd think he was something worse, and she'd be right.

"Danny?" Ann said. "Just tell her."

Danny let out a long breath and sat on a bale of hay. He took off his hat and held it in his hands. And told her the story.

"I went right back to look for him the next day. But he was gone. Worst thing I've ever done in my life."

Ann knelt and put her hand on his wrist. "Don't be so hard on yourself, Danny."

"How could you *do* that?" Meg spat. "You don't just go out and leave your dog alone in the wild."

Danny looked up and said, "It was either that or kill him!"

Meg's eyes narrowed, but she didn't walk away. "You could have found him a home. A ton of people would have taken a dog in, 'specially a sweet one like that."

"I tried! But no one would take a dog who chases stock. I only had one day. I . . . tried. So did my brother, Tyrell, and Ricky."

Ann said, "Give him a chance, Meg. Danny's not the kind of person who'd harm any animal."

"Course not," Danny said. "I had to do it . . . to save his life."

Nobody spoke.

Danny stood. "Where is he?"

"At home."

"Can I see him?"

Meg squinted, her eyes boring into his. Then, "Okay . . . but on one condition. . . . You don't get to take him. Not yet."

Danny slapped his hat against his thigh. "I'm not so sure he'd want me to, anyway."

54

Meg felt the sadness in Danny's voice and in the way he'd tried to explain things.

"Well," she said softly, "I'd better go. My family's here."

The crowd set off a sudden earthquake of roaring and stomping in the stands. Danny said, "Maybe we could set up a time for me to come out to your place . . . if that's . . . all right with you."

"How about right after the rodeo?" Ann said.

Meg took her time answering. "Sure . . . why not?"

"Perfect!" Ann said. "That okay with you, Danny?"

He looked down and dug a small trench in the dirt with the heel of his boot, shaking his head. "I'll ask. But before I go anywhere I've got something to square with my dad. I'll find you later . . . if I'm still alive."

55

The team-roping event began with a red-hot pair from Llano, Texas. Wham! Bam! Done!

They'd be hard to beat.

Danny stood with his hand under Pete's chin, stroking his cheek on the far side. When their time came, he mounted and rode out into the arena, a half horse-length behind Dad, who had yet to say a word to him.

The muscles in Danny's jaw were tight. He'd had back-to-back worst days. Lie after lie. It made his hands shake.

When they got to the box, they turned the horses toward the arena and backed them in, Danny on Pete to the left of the chute, Dad on Mandingo to the right.

As Danny built his loop, he glanced at the chute between them. Their steer looked decent. He was thankful for that.

He jiggled the reins lightly, and Pete backed farther into the box.

Header and heeler took note of each other, then focused in on what they were doing now and what they were about to do.

Pete was jacked up and ready, his flank taut. Danny's hand would tell him when to move. He knew Pete would be screaming to fly out of the box when the gate opened. But he wouldn't move until Danny gave him the signal.

Danny took one last quick glance to see if Dad was ready. He would not look at or think about him again. If Dad had a problem, he'd call it out.

Concentrate. This one last time.

His team roping days with Dad would crash and burn after this. His lies had killed the trust.

He had to do well. He owed it to Dad. In all their time together, Dad had never once missed catching both heels. He was 100 percent, and proud of it, though he'd never admit it.

Danny wasn't about to mess him up now.

The steer's head was not quite forward.

Turn, Danny willed. *Face the front of the chute.*

Pete quivered like a drawn bow.

Danny leaned forward, coiled rope in his left hand, built loop in his right.

When the steer faced front, Danny nodded.

The gatekeeper slammed open the gate.

The steer burst out and raced into the arena.

Pete jumped ahead, slightly. Danny held until the steer broke the barrier, then flew out after him.

Mandingo burst out a split second later, Dad leaning ahead, riding off the steer's right shoulder, hazing him left.

Danny rode the left hindquarters, about four feet to the side of the steer. He leaned forward with the rope whirling over his head, focusing on the steer's left horn, where the loop would end up.

One swing, two.

He threw.

It landed perfectly over both horns. He pulled the slack straight back and made his dally around the saddle horn and pulled the steer to the left, trying to make him hop so Dad could get a good shot at his heels.

Dad threw his loop . . . caught one foot . . . wrapped his rope around the saddle horn, and pulled up on Mandingo.

Danny turned Pete and faced the steer with his rope taut.

It was over.

At the signal from the flagger they slacked up and un-dallied their wrapped ropes. Two wranglers ran out and released the steer.

The Mack team rode out of the arena at a trot, fans clapping politely.

A good show, but not good enough.

The one-heel catch earned them a five-second penalty. They came in second to last, last being a team that had missed the heels altogether.

Danny felt sick.

56

Three-quarters of an hour later, Pete and Mandingo were in the two-horse trailer starting for home with Dad.

Danny had tried to say how sorry he was for lying, but he'd only gotten two words out before Dad raised his hand. "You've got nothing to say that I want to hear."

Tyrell kept his mouth shut as he helped load the horses.

He and Danny watched Dad drive away, the trailer swaying over the dirt.

"Little brother?"

Danny stared after the truck.

"I were you, I'd just keep my mouth shut till he's ready to talk."

"Nothing he could say would make me feel any worse than I already do."

They headed for the stands.

"Danny! Tyrell!"

They turned and saw Ann waving them up. "You go on," Tyrell said. "I need some water."

Danny took the steps two at a time.

A man shouted, "Nice roping, kid," and Danny nodded, thanking him.

Ann was sitting with Meg and what looked like her

family. Danny recognized the tall guy. Another kid sat on the other side of him, the two of them looking as friendly as wolves.

Ann scooted over and patted a spot next to her.

Danny sat.

"Danny," Meg said. "This is my mom and dad and my brothers Jacob and Jeremy."

Danny glanced over at them and nodded. "Hello."

The mother had a nice smile, and the dad didn't look too put out about anything. But the brothers sure did. He wanted to ask Meg what their problem was. Instead he said, "Uh . . . about Banjo, should—"

Ann touched his arm. "We've got it all worked out. We'll go right after the rodeo."

"I just want to see Banjo and know that he's okay." He looked at his hands, then at Meg. "Thanks for taking care of him. He's a . . . a good dog and—"

Danny stopped. He glanced toward the concessions. *Hurry up, Tyrell.* The girl and her brothers made him nervous.

"Meg," Ann said. "How interested are you in staying to the end of this?"

"Not too much, I guess. Why?"

"Well, maybe we could go see Danny's dog now."

"Sure . . . if it's okay with my brother and my mom. We brought two cars."

Mrs. Harris shielded her eyes from the sun, looking over at Danny. "Okay, but you ride with Jacob, since I don't know Danny and his brother. That okay with you, Jacob?"

"Sure," he said.

· · ·

Tyrell, Danny, and Ann followed Jacob's truck.

"You sure you want to do this?" Tyrell said. "You know it will only make it harder on you."

Danny looked out the window. "I'm sure."

But he wasn't.

"Those people didn't look too happy to know the famous Danny Mack."

"I know," Ann said. "It was weird."

"They think I dumped Banjo."

Tyrell mumbled, "We did dump him."

A while later, they slowed and drove down a long gravel drive.

"Wow," Tyrell said. "This is the kind of place you dream about."

Two horses in a paddock that ran alongside the drive followed Jacob's truck as they drove in.

In a pen beyond, Danny spotted a lone bay horse watching them. The horse was on the small side but handsome.

In the side-view mirror, he noticed a shiny black big-wheeled pickup following them down the drive. He turned to Tyrell.

"I see him," Tyrell said.

Jacob parked by the barn.

Tyrell pulled up nearby.

The guy in the black truck parked behind Tyrell and got out.

With a rifle.

57

They watched the guy in the mirror. Tyrell said, "Feels like we're walking into trouble."

But the guy waved at Jacob and Meg and headed around behind the barn.

Tyrell, Danny, and Ann got out.

Meg watched Danny, liking the way he took his time, his quiet manner. When he'd met her parents, he was thoughtful and polite. Which made the whole thing with Banjo more confusing.

"Nice place," Danny said, walking up.

"He's in the barn."

She hadn't meant to be that rude. She softened her tone. "At . . . at least, he usually is. We don't keep him tied up."

"I never did, either."

The two of them went into the barn.

Banjo was in the back corner of one of the horse stalls and appeared to be asleep. "I made him a bed of hay," Meg said. "He's been depressed."

Banjo raised his head, and when he saw Danny, his eyes shifted away, as if guilty.

Meg's throat tightened. *This is so sad. Banjo should have jumped up and run to him. Or at least wagged his tail.*

There was no way she was giving him back unless she saw good reason to, and right now that wasn't happening.

Danny dropped to his knees. "Banjo," he said softly.

Banjo struggled up and moved away from Danny.

"It's okay, boy," Danny whispered. "I'm not gonna hurt you. I know you're a . . . a good dog."

Banjo dipped his head and let out a low whine. He dragged himself back toward Danny on his belly.

Tears rushed into Meg's eyes.

Bam!

The gunshot echoed through the barn.

Banjo scrambled up and cowered in the corner, trembling.

"No!" Meg ran out, yelling, "Dex, no!"

Danny leaped to his feet.

A second shot was followed by the clinking sound of a tumbling can.

Banjo circled the stall, then ran out.

Bam!

Another can clinked.

"Dex!" Meg shouted. "Stop shooting!"

Danny chased after Banjo, now running crazed, head and tail low, looking for a way out of the barn. He clipped Meg, sending her to her knees.

Meg scrambled back up, and together she and Danny managed to grab him and hold him close, Banjo struggling, trying to escape, eyes bulging.

Danny wiped his eyes on the shoulders of his shirt.

Meg took Banjo's head in her hands. "It's over, Banjo, it's over, it's over."

58

"Guns scare him," Meg said softly.

"They should."

Ann, Jacob, and Tyrell ran into the barn. Tyrell crouched next to Danny and Banjo. "He okay?"

Danny shook his head. "He may never be okay again, after what he's been through."

"The gunshots . . . ," Meg said.

Jacob turned to head out. "I'll tell Dex to stop."

"I already did."

Jacob touched Meg. "Some man just called the house. He said he knew the dog."

Danny's head snapped up. "What man?"

"Didn't say. Just told him he'd better get over here, because there's someone else knows the dog, too."

Danny stood. "He's coming now?"

"As we speak."

"Jacob," Meg said. "Why—"

"You said you wanted to find the owner, didn't you? Isn't that why we put up all those signs?" Jacob lifted his chin toward Danny. "How do we know it's his dog? Maybe it's the other guy's."

Ann touched his arm. "I know Banjo is Danny's dog, Jacob."

Jacob nodded. "Okay, but the guy's still coming over."

Danny felt the back of his neck bristle. Had to be Mr. Brodie. Who else? "I know who it is, and he doesn't want to claim Banjo. He wants to take him away and put him down."

Jacob snorted.

"It's true," Tyrell said. "He's our neighbor, and he's not giving up."

"So what can we do?" Meg asked.

Danny shook his head. "I've about run out of ideas."

Meg looked toward the barn door. "We have to hide him. Now!"

"Put him in your truck, Tyrell," Ann said. "Let's just get him out of here."

Danny put up a hand. "No. I'm done lying. I'll deal with whatever comes, but I'll tell you this, he's not taking Banjo."

Meg moved up next to him. "He's going to have to get by me, too."

Dex appeared in the barn door. "Some old coot just drove up looking for Meg."

59

Mr. Brodie had come alone. He stood by his truck with his hands in the pockets of his dusty coveralls. He studied Danny a moment, then turned away.

"I come about the dog," he said. He took one of Meg's posters from his pocket and peeled it open. "Which one of you girls is Meg Harris?"

Meg nodded.

He tapped the poster. "If this is the dog I think it is, and judging by who's standing next to you, I'm right, then it's wanted by the law."

Jacob barked out a laugh. "Seriously? The *dog* is wanted by the law?"

Mr. Brodie kept his eyes on Meg. "Where is he, miss?"

Danny stepped closer. "He's in the barn, Mr. Brodie."

Mr. Brodie's eyes shifted from Meg to Danny. "How's your new pup doing?"

Danny blinked but said nothing.

Mr. Brodie sighed. "Listen. We can do this the easy way, or we can do it the hard way."

"Now, wait a minute," Jacob said, moving in. "Is that a threat? Because if it is, I'm going to ask you to leave."

"All's I want is to get that dog impounded, son. It was

attacking my livestock. He pointed toward the horses out in the pasture. "You got stock. You must understand that."

"He hasn't bothered any of our animals," Meg said. "Why's that?"

Mr. Brodie nodded. "Maybe so, but my boys caught him going after mine, and I don't aim to see him come back to do it again."

"He's not coming back, Mr. Brodie," Danny said. "I know the law, but I don't believe he did what Billy and Ben said he did. Banjo's not that kind of dog, and I'm not going to let you take him."

Mr. Brodie squinted at Danny a long moment, then turned toward his truck. "Be back soon, folks. Don't go nowhere."

Mr. Brodie drove off.

Ann said, "He wouldn't kill Banjo . . . would he?"

"Maybe not personally," Tyrell said, "but he'd have the law do it. You remember the collie-malamute that chased that woman's horse and got taken to court? It was all over the papers."

"I remember," Jacob said.

"He was sentenced to die," Tyrell went on. "But he got lucky and was sent to some shelter in Utah for wayward animals. The lady who owned the horse wasn't too happy about that, but they got it worked out. Banjo might not be so lucky."

"But Banjo's not a killer," Meg said.

"This guy caught him going after what?" Jacob asked. "Cattle?"

"Sheep," Tyrell said.

Danny paced. "Problem is, you have to protect your livestock. A pack of wild dogs can do more damage than wolves."

"Banjo was running with wild dogs?"

"At night. That's what that old guy's boys say."

"But why would he?" Meg said. "He's not wild."

Danny crossed his arms and looked at his boots. "Alls I know is ranchers see their calves and sheep dying, and how they deal with it is they shoot, right then. And it's legal."

"Dogs don't know right from wrong," Meg said. "They live in a different world. Like horses, and birds. Like any animal."

"I just don't want my dog shot," Danny said.

Meg stared at Danny. "I'd say he's not your dog anymore."

Danny sat on the ground next to Banjo. His gut was tight as a whip, and his fingers trembled.

"So now what?" Meg asked.

Danny shook his head.

60

Less than an hour later, they were all over by the barn as Mr. Brodie drove up, trailed by an Oregon state trooper.

"You want me to handle this, Danny?" Tyrell asked.

"I can do it. But thanks."

"Got your back."

Mr. Brodie and the trooper parked and got out. "That's the boy owns the dog," Mr. Brodie said. "And that's the girl who found him. This is her place."

The trooper looked at Meg. "Your parents home, miss?"

Meg shook her head.

"Don't matter if they are or they're not," Mr. Brodie said. "It's the dog we're talking about, the one attacked my sheep. It's here, somewhere."

Danny sprang forward, inches from Mr. Brodie's face. "He didn't attack your sheep! I *know* my dog."

The trooper motioned for Danny to step back. "I need to see the dog. And I need to take him with me." His eyes shifted to Meg. "When do you expect your parents?"

"They—"

Bam!

The trooper flinched, his hand swinging to his sidearm.

"It's okay, "Jacob said. "Just a friend shooting cans."

When a second shot rang out, Danny backed away and ran toward the barn.

"Wait!" Meg called, and ran after him.

Banjo was gone.

"How'd he get out?" Meg said. "The stall door was closed!"

Danny ran to the pasture behind the barn.

"Banjo!"

Meg followed, shouting over to Dex, who stood with his rifle crooked in his arms. "What's *wrong* with you? The dog is scared of gunshots! I *told* you that!"

Mr. Brodie, the trooper, Ann, Tyrell, and Jacob all came through the barn and out into the sunlight.

"He lit on out," Dex said, waving toward the trees.

"What's going on here?" the trooper said.

Meg glared at Dex. "The shots scared him off."

Dex pointed with his chin. "Ran that way."

Danny took off across the pasture, heading for the trees.

"Okay," the trooper said. "Let's all fan out and see if we can get him back."

They searched for a full hour with no trace of Banjo. By the time everyone but Danny had straggled back, the rest of Meg's family had returned from the rodeo.

"What's going on, Jacob?" Mr. Harris asked.

Jacob nodded toward the trooper. "He's here to take Banjo away."

"Why?" Mrs. Harris asked.

The trooper introduced himself and motioned to Mr. Brodie. "This is Mr. Brodie from Redmond. He's filed a complaint, charging the dog with attacking his sheep. I'm sorry, but I have to take him away, at least until this matter is settled."

"I know the livestock predator law," Mrs. Harris said. "But you're wrong about this dog."

She went on to say they'd get Banjo a lawyer and take it to court.

The trooper advised against it. "The law is there for a reason, Mrs. Harris. Something like this isn't easy for anyone."

"It's a bad law . . . in this case."

They turned toward the barn when Danny emerged and strode toward them, head down, hat hiding his face. "Banjo's gone."

The trooper thought a moment, then turned to Mr. Brodie. "Not much I can do now."

Mr. Brodie nodded. "I understand."

The trooper took a card from his shirt pocket and handed it to Mr. Harris. "Give me a call when the dog comes back."

Danny kicked the dirt and walked away.

61

Mr. Brodie and the trooper drove off.

Danny felt light-headed, almost dizzy. *Get a grip. Banjo is still alive. Somewhere out there.*

Meg's parents linked hands and headed into the house.

Jeremy went out back with Dex.

Danny looked into the distance at the trees and mountains. *Keep running, bud. Find a safe home with a good family . . . somewhere.*

"You all right?" Meg asked.

"Yeah . . . no . . . I'm not."

Ann, Jacob, Tyrell, Meg, and Danny walked over to the pasture and hung their arms over the fence. Molly and Sunspot looked back at them from across the way.

Meg flinched when Dex slid in next to her. "Come," he said. "I want to show you something."

"Not interested."

"You *want* to see this."

Dex led them to the gallery of mangled shot-up cans, which he and Jeremy had realigned on the bales of hay. A small mountain of additional bales was stacked farther back to catch stray bullets. "What do you see?"

"Nothing."

Dex grinned and dragged two of the bales away, revealing a dark cave-like interior. "He may be scared, but he's not in that cop's car."

"You *hid* Banjo?"

Danny and Meg crouched and looked in. A low whine came from the back.

"I heard you talking out there," Dex said. "I know what that geezer wanted."

Danny called into the dark hollow. "Banjo. Come on out, boy."

Banjo limped out. How old and tired his dog seemed! "I'm so sorry, bud . . . I'm so, so sorry." He hugged him.

Dex crouched beside Danny. "That's a real good dog."

"I know," Danny said. "And he shouldn't have to suffer like this."

"Sorry I had to scare him."

Danny stood and reached down to give Dex a hand up. "Thanks, friend. You may have saved his life."

"I'm going to regret this later," Meg said. "But, Dexter—nice going."

"Holy haystack! She has a heart."

"And I have an idea," Danny said.

62

Banjo stood in Danny's lap, his head out the window.

The sun was on its westward slide, but there were still a few hours of daylight left.

Danny and Tyrell had dropped Ann off at her apartment and were now easing down a potholed street in an old section of Bend, looking for Spike's house. They had to swerve a time or two to avoid loose dogs, a lazy cat, and a tricycle abandoned in the middle of the road.

Danny had talked Meg into letting him give his plan a try. Now that the law was involved, she'd have to give Banjo up. So what was there to lose?

Tyrell lifted his chin. "There."

Spike's house looked completely out of place. It was freshly painted. The grass was green and cut in neat rows. Flowers lined the walkway to the front door.

Danny put his hat on and got out. He took Banjo's leash and hooked it to his collar. Banjo jumped out and headed for the grass. Danny let him sniff and inspect and pee.

They headed up the path.

"Sure hope this works," Tyrell said.

"It's got to."

Tyrell rang the doorbell and stepped back.

A woman opened the door. A smile grew on her face. "Well, well, it's the famous Tyrell."

"Hi, Janey."

"And who's this handsome young man?"

"My brother, Danny, only don't call him handsome. His head is too big as it is."

Danny shoved Tyrell.

"And he's violent."

Janey reached out and shook Danny's hand. "Nice to meet you, Danny."

Danny smiled. "Is Spike home?"

"He sure is. Come on in."

Danny looked down at Banjo. "I'll stay outside with him."

Janey crouched down and took Banjo's face in her hands. "And who are you?" She scratched behind his ears. Banjo kissed her with his wet nose.

"My dog, Banjo."

Janey looked up and smiled. "I don't mind a dog in the house. Come on in. I'll get Spike."

They waited just inside the door.

Danny thought Spike would probably have a Harley parked in his living room, with parts spread out on a mat. And the whole house would smell like oil and gas.

But the house was bright and clean and smelled like roses.

Tyrell leaned close to Danny's ear. "She probably makes Spike soak his fingernails in bleach every night after work."

Danny smiled.

"Heyyy, my men," Spike said, drying his hands with a paper towel. "To what do I owe this dubious honor?"

Danny cocked his head. "What?"

Spike grinned. "Thought I was just an ex-thief and a grease monkey, huh?"

"No, I—"

"Well I am. What's this?" He squatted down to scratch Banjo's chin. "Where's the fleabite you brought in the other day? What's the name? Ruby?"

"Yeah, Ruby."

"And this is?"

"Banjo," Danny said, looking down at his dog.

"*This* is Banjo? I thought you said . . ."

"It's a long story."

"I've got time."

"Spike, *please,* can you take Banjo to California with you? You've got to, Spike. I know Tyrell said you wouldn't, but this isn't a joke. I'm telling you, if I don't get him out of this state, he'll be taken away, maybe even killed."

As Danny told the story, Spike looked from Danny to Tyrell to Banjo.

"He's been through a lot, Spike, and none of it was his fault. . . . He . . . he barely trusts me anymore, and now gunshots scare him, when they didn't used to."

"Why me, Danny?"

"Well . . . first of all, I trust you. Second, you like dogs. Third, you're going far away, and Banjo can't stay anywhere near here. And fourth . . . well, you *do* always talk about how you miss Grouch."

Spike nodded. "Grouch."

He squatted and called Banjo close. "And what do you have to say about this?"

Banjo licked Spike's face.

"Janey," Spike called. "Come here a sec."

She came back holding a roll of packing tape.

"Danny is in dire need of saving this dog's life by finding him a home. He's been accused of chasing the neighbor's sheep, and around here they shoot dogs that—"

"Yes," she said.

"What?"

"It's time, Spike. Yes, we'll take him. I heard it all."

Banjo sat panting.

Janey knelt down next to Spike and reached out to Banjo.

Banjo's tail thumped on the floor. He scooted closer and licked Janey's hand, then her face. Though a lump burned in Danny's throat at the thought of giving Banjo away, he could see that Banjo liked both of them, and he couldn't think of anyone better than Spike and Janey to protect him.

"Grouch would be okay with this," Janey said.

A crooked grin grew on Spike's face. He looked up at Danny and Tyrell. "Ain't she the best? Don't you fret one more minute, my friends. This dog is now in safe hands."

"*Yes!*" Danny said. "Yes, yes, yes! Thank you!"

Spike stood, and Danny nearly shook his hand right off his arm.

Janey hugged him.

"One more thing, Spike," Danny said. He looked out the window. The sun was low, but there was still a good amount of daylight left. "Can you take a ride with us? Unless you have other plans."

"Where to?"

"Yeah," Tyrell said. "Where?"

Danny had thought about this ever since they'd left Meg's place. If Spike said yes, he'd do it. "To see Mr. Brodie . . . the guy who wants Banjo shot."

Tyrell looked at Danny as if he was crazy. "What for?"

"I've . . . I've got to get my dignity back, Tyrell."

Spike grinned. "Your wheels or mine, partner?"

63

Danny, riding with Spike, watched Tyrell following in the side-view mirror. He loved his brother. He was always there when Danny needed him. Danny hoped he'd never let Tyrell down when there was something he needed. Letting Dad down was about as much as he could ever take. He was done with lies and deception.

The Brodie house was in the lowlands, not too far from the grassy rise where Billy Brodie had made the shot that sent Danny's world spinning.

Danny pointed to the hillside that led up to his own place. "We live just over there."

"Nice country out here."

Spike parked near Mr. Brodie's truck. Tyrell pulled in behind him. Before they'd even opened their doors, Mr. Brodie stepped out onto the veranda.

"That him?" Spike asked.

"Yep."

Mr. Brodie studied them with his hands in the pockets of his coveralls.

Banjo, who was sitting on Danny's lap, stuck his head out the window.

"He sees the dog," Spike said.

"I want him to."

Mr. Brodie stepped down off the porch.

Spike raised his eyebrows. "This is going to be interesting."

They all got out.

Danny set Banjo in the bed of Spike's truck, where he whined at Mr. Brodie's barking dogs, fenced off out of sight.

The Brodie boys appeared from the barn.

"See you found your dog," Mr. Brodie said.

Danny kept his eyes off Billy and Ben. He stood tall and faced Mr. Brodie. "Mr. Brodie . . . I've lied to you, and I've lied to my dad. After you came over and said my dog attacked your sheep, I told him I'd put Banjo down myself. He didn't think it was a good idea, but he let me have it my way. But I didn't. I . . . couldn't."

Danny looked down at his hands, then leveled his gaze. "I tried to run Banjo off, far from here . . . so I could . . . keep him alive."

Danny had to look away, curbing his emotions. "It was wrong of me, sir. I know that now. But I still don't believe my dog—"

"I asked you once today how the pup was," Mr. Brodie interrupted. "You never did tell me."

"What?"

"The pup. How is she?"

"She's . . . fine. And smart. I'm . . . well, I'm getting her used to being around the steers right now."

Mr. Brodie nodded. "She'll be running them around like a cuttin' horse before you know it."

Danny's confession was set off track, now. This wasn't how he'd seen it in his mind. Mr. Brodie seemed . . . different.

Spike's gaze shifted. "That an old Honda you got over there?"

They all turned and looked at the red motorcycle leaning against the barn.

"Piece of junk," Ben said.

Billy snorted. "Barely good enough to sell for parts."

Mr. Brodie squinted at them. "Bike's not yours to sell, now, is it?"

Billy's face reddened.

Mr. Brodie turned back to Spike. "That old Honda broke down on me about six months back. She was good for about ten years. Now we use a four-wheeler to get around the place."

"Mind if I take a look?"

"Key's in it, but it don't work."

Tyrell looked at Danny and shrugged.

As they all walked over to the Honda, Tyrell introduced Mr. Brodie to Spike. "We work together at Les Schwab's, in Sisters."

"That so," Mr. Brodie said.

Spike rolled the Honda away from the barn and kicked out its stand. He crouched low and examined it.

Danny didn't know if it was good or bad to have his confession put on hold so everybody could look at a broke-down motorbike.

Spike poked around the engine. "You got a small screw-driver?"

"In the house," Mr. Brodie said. He nodded for Ben to run and get it.

Danny frowned. This was crazy. Spike knew why they'd come here.

Ben came back with the screwdriver. Spike took it and removed a small hose. He ran the hose between his fingers, then put it to his lips and blew on it. His cheeks puffed up and his face went red. A moment later a glob of gunk flew out the open end of the tubing.

Spike spat and screwed the tubing back on the cycle. "Fuel line was clogged. Let's see if she works now."

He kicked it over. On the fifth try, the Honda sputtered to life.

"I'll be danged," Mr. Brodie said.

Spike gunned the engine, two, three, four times. "Man, I love that sound, don't you?" He smiled and took the Honda out and back on a short smoky spin. He shut it down and sat on it. "Good as new."

Mr. Brodie scratched the back of his neck. "I thank you for bringing her back to me, Spike."

"My pleasure."

"Now," Mr. Brodie said. "What was it y'all come to see me about, besides confessing?"

Billy cracked up. Ben furrowed his brow, confused.

Spike said, "Mr. Brodie, Danny would like you to give his dog another chance by letting me take him to California. My wife and I are moving, and we could give him a good home. Simple as that."

Mr. Brodie studied Spike, then Danny. "Why'nt you just take him? I'd of never known it. I thought the dog was gone, anyway."

Spike got off the bike and put a hand on Danny's shoulder.

"Because Danny's a good kid, and he's no liar. He wanted to square things up."

Danny tried as hard as he could to hold Mr. Brodie's gaze.

"What dog are we talking about, now?" Mr. Brodie asked.

Spike looked back at Banjo. "That one. Over there in my truck."

"I don't see no dog."

They all looked at Banjo, who was watching them.

Spike said, "I could've sworn there was a dog in my truck."

"How about you, Danny?" Mr. Brodie said. "You see one?"

"No, sir, I guess I don't."

64

When they got home, Tyrell turned off the engine but didn't get out. *"Star Wars,"* he said, turning to Danny. *"Rogue One.* Remember that scene at the end. Darth Vader shows up out of nowhere and takes on a whole mess of rebel fighters after they steal the Death Star plans? Wham! Bam! Boom! Wipes them all out? Remember that?"

"What are you talking about?"

Tyrell sat back. "Man, he was scary. Remember when he went ballistic?"

"Well . . . yeah."

"So that's what you're stressing about, right? Going in to face Darth Vader?"

"This is serious, Tyrell. He's going to kill me!"

"No . . . he's not."

"Yes, he is! I lied to him. He trusted me, and I blew it. And I ruined his roping record at the rodeo." Danny covered his face with his hands.

"I'm as guilty as you are," Tyrell said softly. "I backed you up on that lie."

Danny shook his head. "No, Tyrell. None of this is your—"

"Yes, it is. Come on, let's go in."

They got out and headed into the house.

Dad was washing dishes, a cup of coffee on the windowsill above the sink.

Danny took off his hat and set it on the kitchen table. He paused and glanced back at Tyrell, who was leaning against the wall with his arms crossed.

Danny turned back. "Dad?"

Dad turned off the water, dried his hands, and grabbed his coffee. "Have a seat," he said, not looking at either of his sons.

Danny eased into a chair at the table. Tyrell stayed where he was.

Dad eyed Tyrell as he pulled out a chair but said nothing as he sat across from Danny. "You go see the dog?"

"Yes, sir."

"Where's he at?"

"With Spike, a guy who works with Tyrell."

Dad glanced over at Tyrell.

"He's taking him to California," Tyrell said. "He and his wife are moving next week."

Danny's heart thumped so hard he worried Dad could hear it.

Dad turned back to Danny. "That's a good solution. But you'll have to square it with Harmon first. He deserves to know. You fooled him just like you fooled me. You need to apologize."

"I just did. That's where me and Tyrell just came from."

"Tyrell and I, not me and Tyrell."

"Tyrell and I."

"What'd he have to say about it?"

"He thought it was a good idea."

Dad's piercing gaze unnerved Danny. He had to look away. *Why doesn't he just yell at me, tell me how disappointed he is, and how lying is a coward's way out, and how he didn't raise me to be of such low character, and why did I do it!*

But Dad said nothing.

Danny couldn't stand it. "Dad, I'll never lie to you again. I promise you. I don't think I've ever felt so bad about anything as I have about that. Once you start lying it's too hard to stop. It's crazy. I know I lost your trust. I know I ruined your roping record. I know it and I'm sorry. I'm really . . . sorry."

Silence.

"Dad?"

"You think that's what this is about? My roping record?"

"Well . . . partly."

Dad stared at him. "My record is nothing, Danny. It's not important at all. What is important is that you didn't trust me enough to tell me you couldn't shoot your dog. I let you go out there because that was your decision. I didn't think you could do it. I was surprised when you told me you did. I was surprised that Tyrell didn't stop you." He turned to Tyrell. "I was also surprised that he played along with your scheme, which is even more . . ."

He didn't go on, just turned away and shook his head.

"Why'd you let me go, then?" Danny said. "If you knew

I wouldn't do it, why'd you say I could?" Danny didn't understand his own feelings right now, almost angry, angry at Dad.

Dad reached over and put his hand on Danny's. "If I made your tough decisions for you, Danny, I'd be doing you a disservice. So I let you take that one on yourself." He looked into Danny's eyes a moment, then took his hand away.

Danny thought about all the decisions he'd made since Billy Brodie shot Banjo. Not all of them were good, but some were. He'd worked it out, maybe not in the best way, but he'd worked it out.

"My decisions were pretty stupid," he said, looking at the table. "I guess I failed that class."

Dad studied Danny a moment, then said, "You never fail, Danny. You win . . . or you learn."

He'd learned, all right. Oh, he had learned. "Yes, sir."

Dad turned to Tyrell.

Tyrell ducked his head, looking as guilty as Danny felt. "I'm sorry, too, Dad. Maybe I could have done it different. I don't know. It was a hard thing to figure out. I didn't want Banjo to die, either. I . . . I had to help Danny."

Dad got up and dumped his coffee in the sink. "You boys disappointed me, sure. But you owned up to it. You squared it with Harmon, and you squared it with me. In fact, you saved Banjo." He turned to Danny and half smiled. "To tell the truth, I'm proud of you, son."

Proud?

Dad put his hands on Danny's shoulders. "Hungry?"

"Always."

Dad looked over at Tyrell and winked. "Let's us men go on over to Bend and have us a good dinner, what do you say?"

Danny pushed his chair out and stood. "Dad, I need you to know that I'm truly sorry for . . . for what I did."

Dad picked up Danny's hat and handed it to him. "I know you are. Now, let's go. I'm starving."

65

ONE WEEK LATER

The following weekend, Tyrell gave Danny a ride to Meg's place.

He glanced over at Danny. "Nervous?"

"No."

"She's a hot wire."

Danny ignored him.

"I can't believe it. Little brother's first girlfriend."

"She's not my girlfriend."

"What are you two gonna do?"

Danny shrugged. "Got any ideas?"

"Well—"

"I'm kidding!"

The radio blasted country music. Ruby stood in his lap, sniffing the crisp air flowing into the cab. Two fly rods rattled in the truck bed.

Tyrell grinned. "Dad's going to love this."

Danny turned and raised a fist.

"Okay, okay, I'll keep my mouth shut. But he's going to find out anyway, and rub it in worse than me. You know that, don't you?"

"Yeah."

"So listen, I'll pick you up around five . . . unless, that is, she sends you packing early." He laughed.

Danny had wondered about that.

The night before, Danny had worked up his nerve and called Meg. He'd told her about Spike taking Banjo, and how it went with Mr. Brodie. He was feeling so good, he asked if he could visit her. He'd been thinking of her constantly, of how she'd cared for Banjo, and how she wasn't about to give him up until she knew he was in good hands. He liked her for that. A lot . . . even though she'd thought he was a skunk.

Meg Harris.

He smiled.

Tyrell drove up the drive. "Look."

Meg was sitting on a bale of hay, reading something with a cat in her lap.

"She's waiting for you. In case you're not picking up on it, that's a good sign."

Danny dried his palms on his jeans as Tyrell pulled up. He tucked Ruby under one arm and got out, jamming her leash in his back pocket.

Meg set the cat down and jumped up. "A puppy!"

Danny handed her over. "Her name's Ruby."

He grabbed the two fishing rigs out of the truck. "Thanks, Tyrell. See you around five."

Tyrell gave Danny and Meg a two-finger salute and drove off.

"She's so cute!" Meg said. "Ruby. What a beautiful name. Where'd you get her?"

"You won't believe this, but Mr. Brodie gave her to me."

"You're *kidding.*"

Danny reached over and scratched Ruby's head. "He lost four sheep to wild dogs and coyotes last year, which is why he was so dead set on going after Banjo. He was just being a rancher. But he felt bad when Dad told him I'd shot my own dog, so he brought Ruby over. His border collie had a litter of 'em."

"I guess you just never know about people, do you?" Meg said.

"Ain't that the truth." Danny thought of what he'd expected at Spike's house. And he'd been wrong about Mr. Brodie, too, and even Dad.

He nodded to the card in her hand. "Mail?"

Meg looked at it, as if just remembering she had it. "Oh. Yeah. It's from my friend Josie. She sent this from Seattle."

Danny nodded. "Been to Seattle once. Big place. Huge."

Meg laughed. "That's just what she wrote on this card. Funny."

They fell silent. Looked at Ruby.

"I miss Banjo," Danny said. "He was the best dog."

"Jacob had a dog once, but he got kicked by one of the horses. It was awful. We never got another one."

"I'm sorry."

"Yeah . . . So what do you want to do?"

"I brought some fly rods. Thought maybe we could find a stream and catch some trout. You like to fish?"

Meg wrinkled her nose.

"What?"

"I don't like to kill things."

"I use barbless hooks and throw them back."

"Do you, now."

He liked the way she was squinting at him, eyes lit up with some kind of mischief.

"Are you a hunter?"

That took Danny by surprise. "Well . . . sure. Everybody hunts. Around here."

"I don't believe people should kill animals. I think it's wrong."

"Okay."

He could live with that.

"What does *okay* mean?" Meg asked.

"Well, I guess it means it's fine with me that you don't believe people should hunt."

"Good."

Meg started over to the arena. "Come."

Danny took Ruby and leashed her. In the arena, the spunky horse watched them approach, head high, ears forward.

"What grade are you in?" Meg asked.

Man, she sure changes directions. "Uh, just finished seventh."

"Hey, me too!"

"Cool."

Meg climbed up on the first rung of the fence and hung her arms over the top. Danny hung his over, too, only he could do it from the ground. His arm brushed hers. They glanced at each other, and heat flushed over Danny's face. But neither of them moved their arm away.

He turned back to the horse. "Mustang?"

"Good eye. I got him over in Prineville from a guy who couldn't handle him. I call him Amigo . . . but he's not all that friendly. I've been working with him, or trying to. He's still got a lot of wild in him."

"So he's not saddle broke?"

"Look at him," Meg said. "He's watching us. No, he's not ready for a saddle. I haven't even put a halter on him. I'm still trying to earn his trust."

Amigo took a few steps closer, following the fence to get a better look at Meg and Danny.

"Mind if I try?" he asked, tying Ruby's leash to the fence.

"Try what?"

"Put a halter on him."

Meg studied Amigo. "Let's both do it. I'll get a halter."

"Get a saddle blanket, too."

She smiled. He didn't know how hard she'd worked just to get close to Amigo. He'd soon find out how wary this horse was. She shrugged. "What's the harm?"

She headed to the barn.

When she came back with the halter and saddle blanket, Danny was out in the arena heading toward Amigo, slow and patient. Meg tossed the saddle blanket on the top rail of the fence.

She crossed her arms and watched.

Amigo eyed Danny, then huffed and burst away, running stiff-legged to the other side.

Meg grinned.

Danny started after him, but Meg called, "I got this."

Danny nodded.

She headed out into the arena. When Amigo stopped to watch her, she angled away, turning her back on him. Amigo tossed his head, keeping his eyes on her.

Danny leaned against the fence.

Meg kept on walking away from Amigo.

After a moment, Amigo started to follow her, neck stretched, head low. When she stopped, Amigo stopped. When she went on, Amigo went on.

Danny smiled. *Something special is going on between those two.*

Meg picked up a handful of dirt, and let it run through her fingers.

Amigo crept closer, sniffing the air. Meg couldn't help but think of the old saying about cats and their curiosity. She grinned. *Come on, Amigo. Investigate.*

Amigo stopped three feet behind her.

Over her shoulder, Meg said, "Don't you worry about that guy over by the fence, Amigo. Just think about you and me. Let's show him what we can do."

Meg eased around to face him. She kept from looking into his eyes, which seemed to be important to him. She walked closer and very slowly reached out to lay her hand on his neck.

Amigo gave a slight flick of his head.

She waited a moment, then stroked and rubbed his cheek. "There we go, now, there we go."

Danny nodded. *Beautiful.*

Meg reached back and pulled the halter from her back

pocket. She held it out for Amigo to sniff. Then she rubbed it along his neck and shoulders, which he didn't seem to mind. "Nothing here to worry about," she whispered.

She stroked Amigo's face and slipped the halter over his ears.

Amigo tossed his head, and she quickly pulled the halter off.

It was the closest she'd ever come.

Danny watched, spellbound. That wild horse could kick a nail into a two-by-four, and there he was accepting Meg's hand.

Meg felt light-headed. *Breathe. Breathe.*

Danny headed over, a huge grin on his face. He stopped halfway and said, low, "He's learning to trust you."

"I know," Meg said, barely loud enough to hear.

Danny's skin tingled. "That was amazing."

She looked at him and almost went over to hug him but caught herself.

Danny looked away. "I'll go get . . . you know . . . the blanket."

"Yeah! The blanket."

He started toward the fence.

"Amigo," Meg whispered. "See that boy? His name is Danny, our new amigo. I think you're going to like him as much as I do."

66

THREE DAYS LATER

It was hot and dry, with no breeze to cool them off.

Danny and Tyrell were doing chores when Tyrell set the wheelbarrow down. He snapped his fingers and nodded toward the west pasture. Two sheep had gotten in. "Brodie boys can't fix a fence for beans."

He and Danny headed out and found another one.

"Wonder if there's more over the ridge," Danny said.

"Let's herd these back and take a look."

Danny whistled for Ruby, who stumbled out from the hay shed. When she saw the sheep, she perked up and ran toward them.

The sheep stirred and hurried back over the ridge.

"Go, Ruby!" Danny called.

Tyrell laughed.

At the top of the rise, Danny and Tyrell looked down at the fence that separated their place from Brodie's. Three more sheep were on their side, grazing on the slope below.

"Ruby, stay!" Danny said.

She sat but kept an eye on the sheep.

Danny and Tyrell separated to funnel them down the rise. As they neared the Brodies' fence, Tyrell stooped and picked something out of the grass.

"What is it?" Danny asked.

Tyrell held it up. Another beer bottle.

"What's going on out here?"

Tyrell sniffed it. "Someone must have come in off the road and passed through."

Danny looked toward the highway, then back over to miles of rolling rangeland to the north. "Passing through to where?"

"Beats me." Tyrell stuck the bottle in his back pocket. "Dad should know people are coming through our pasture."

Danny frowned. "That just doesn't make sense. There's nowhere to go."

Tyrell shrugged.

They continued herding the sheep toward the fence.

"Looks like they broke out in the same spot as the last two times," Tyrell said.

The wire had come loose and was bowed out where dogs or coyotes had dug under it. Danny put his hands on his hips. "Maybe it would be better if we just fixed it for them."

"Let's do it. That loose spot's probably how Banjo and those dogs got in."

"Nope," Danny said.

Tyrell looked at him. "What does that mean?"

"Banjo didn't chase Brodie's sheep."

"He must have been doing *something* over there."

Danny jammed his hands in his pockets.

Tyrell turned to head back up the hill. "Get those sheep through the fence. I'll grab some tools."

It took some doing, but Danny got them all through. As he stood waiting for Tyrell, he noticed the remains of a small campfire near a rock outcropping on the Brodie side. He frowned. Even though it seemed to have been properly put out, making fires in this dry country was not a good idea.

Still . . .

A campfire? Here?

*　*　*

They were installing new clips on a green metal post when the Brodie boys came bouncing through the pasture in their ATV.

Billy jumped out and reached back for his rifle. "What are you doing? That's our fence."

Tyrell said, "Why, that's a mighty neighborly greeting there, Billy boy."

Ben squeezed out of the ATV. "Hey, Danny, Tyrell. What are you doing to our fence?"

"Far as I can tell, there's a hole in it. Am I wrong about that, Danny?"

"Nope."

"One more time," Billy said. "What are you doing?"

Danny threw another shovel of dirt into the hole under

the fence. Then another. Something was eating at him, an idea, a thought. He could feel heat rising in his neck.

Tyrell dropped a large rock on the dirt, blocking the hole. "Your sheep got through again. That makes three times in six months. Same hole. Probably the same sheep." He looked across the fence at Billy. "Someone had to fix it right."

Billy's face reddened. "You saying we didn't?"

"That's what I'm saying."

"That's probably how your dog got in," Ben said.

"You mean that one?" Danny nodded toward Ruby sitting up on the rise.

Tyrell laughed.

Billy held the rifle across his chest. "Pretty sneaky how you tricked our old man into letting your dog off like he did."

Danny was getting it now. The campfire. The empty beer bottles.

He stabbed the shovel into the ground and glared across the fence. "My dog didn't chase anything, did he, Billy? You made that up, didn't you?"

"It's true!" Billy said. "He attacked our sheep! He was with a pack of wild dogs."

Danny glared at him. "You lied to your dad."

Billy stepped closer to the fence. "Who lied to whose dad?"

Danny nearly exploded. But Billy was right.

Ben shouldered in next to his brother. "Your dog was . . . was attacking our sheep . . . right up there on that hill, and . . . and Billy winged him, right, Billy?"

Billy elbowed Ben: *Shut up.*

"Ow!"

Danny kept his eyes on Billy. "That's the same story you told the first time. I missed it then, but Ben just now laid it out. You shot Banjo on the hillside, which is on our side of the fence. So how could he chase your sheep? He wasn't even in your pasture."

Billy's mouth pinched tight. His face reddened.

Danny turned to Tyrell. "Show him what you found."

Tyrell gave Danny a look, then he nodded. He took the bottle from his back pocket and held it up.

Billy's jaw dropped, just slightly.

That was all Danny needed. He knew it! He had it right. He could feel blood pulsing in his temples. "You two snuck out here in the middle of the night. You made a campfire, right over there . . . and you sneaked out some of your dad's beer. Then you thought it would be fun to toss the bottles over to our place. That's it, isn't it, Billy?"

Ben looked at Billy.

Billy's eyes were glued to Danny's. "That's a crock."

Danny wasn't done. "You had your rifle. Maybe you brought it with you for cougars, or Big Foot, but you saw Banjo up there on the rise, just sitting there trying to see what was going on, and you thought it would be fun to take a shot at him. That's what happened."

Billy took a step back. "You don't know what you're talking about."

Ben looked away.

"Look at them squirm," Tyrell said. "You're calling this one right, Danny."

199

Billy spat. "Come on, Ben. Let's get out of here."

They started toward the ATV.

"Hold on," Tyrell said. "Come here a minute."

They stopped and looked back.

"What for?" Billy said.

"I want to see that rifle."

Billy snorted. "Ain't going to happen."

"No, really. There's something wrong with it. I don't want you to get hurt."

Billy looked at the rifle.

"Give it to me," Tyrell said. "I'll show you."

Billy hesitated, then handed the rifle over the fence. "What's wrong with it?"

Tyrell studied it, turning it in his hands. "Your dad's rifle, right?"

"So?"

Tyrell handed it to Danny. "What do you think?"

"Hey," Billy said. "Give that back."

Danny inspected it and handed it back to Tyrell. "Someone could get hurt, all right."

"That's what I thought."

"Give me the rifle!"

Ben moved closer. "So what's wrong with it?"

"Nothing," Billy barked. "And now he's going to give it back."

Tyrell shook his head. "Can't do that. A firearm in the hands of someone who doesn't know how to use it is dangerous. Am I right, Danny?"

Danny kept his eyes on Billy. "Yep."

The veins in Billy's neck bulged. "Give that back! Right now, or I'm taking it."

Danny picked up the shovel and rested it on his shoulders like a baseball bat. "You want it back, you can have it. But your dad has to come for it, not you, and when he does, I'm going to tell him how you lied about my dog, and how you would have let Banjo *die* to hide what you and Ben were doing out here. You *shot* him! Don't you care?"

Ben looked at the ground.

"You're going to pay for this," Billy said.

"No. *You* are!"

"We're done here," Tyrell said. "Let's go home."

Danny nodded but didn't move until the ATV fired up and the brothers took off.

Tyrell put his arm around Danny's shoulder. "You should think about being a detective. That was incredible, the way you put all that together."

"Those two were out here being stupid, and when they shot Banjo, they had to come up with a story or get in trouble for sneaking out."

"And they were willing to let Banjo die rather than tell the truth."

Danny looked up the rise at Ruby. "Banjo suffered . . . for nothing. *Nothing!*"

They headed back up the hill.

"So," Tyrell said as they neared the barn. "What are we going to tell Mr. Brodie when he comes for his rifle? You know he will."

Danny thought a moment. "Well, we'll give it to him . . .

along with that beer bottle and the other one. Let him put two and two together."

Tyrell broke into a wide grin. "You *are* smarter than you look."

"Didn't take a genius."

They headed toward the house, a cow bellowing in the distance.

"Banjo was a good dog, wasn't he?" Tyrell said.

"Still is."

"Yeah. With a good home."

"I miss him, Tyrell."

"You want to try to get him back?"

Danny didn't answer right away. Did he? Of course he did. But what he wanted didn't matter. Only Banjo mattered. And after what they'd done to him . . .

"No," Danny said softly.

"Yeah . . . He'd probably never trust us again."

Danny looked back toward the ridge. He whistled, and Ruby ran over, tripping through the long grass. Danny handed the shovel to Tyrell, picked her up, and tucked her under his arm. "You're a good dog, too."

Ruby panted. Her ears perked.

"Not the same," Tyrell said. "But just as good."

Danny hugged Ruby. "Just as good."

When they got to the house, they went in and turned on every light. That's what they did when Dad was on the road. "What's for dinner?" Danny asked.

"Beans."

"From a can?"

"What do you think?"

Danny got the plates.

They ate, did their chores, fed Ruby, and went to bed.

. . .

In the morning, they got up, ate leftover beans, and went out to do it all over again.

After lunch, Danny called Meg while Tyrell cleaned up.

"Hey," she said.

"How's Amigo?"

"Getting gentler by the day."

Danny closed his eyes, picturing her. "You got a minute? I want to tell you a story."

"What's it about?"

"Banjo . . . the part you don't know."

"Is it better than the part I do know?"

"The guy we got him from said he was once wild. He was nervous around people and skittish."

There was a moment of silence.

"Like Amigo," Meg said.

"Yeah."

More silence.

"And you . . . had to earn his trust?"

"It didn't take as long as Amigo will, but yeah."

"Is that the whole story?"

"Almost."

She laughed. "So what's the rest of it?"

"I'll tell you. But first . . . well . . . do you . . . I mean . . .

after everything that's happened, do you think you can learn to . . . to trust me?"

"It depends."

"On what?"

"On how long it takes you to come over so I can say yes."

Danny covered the phone with his hand. *"Tyrell!"*

Epilogue

At nine o'clock Saturday morning, Danny, Tyrell, and Dad were in the yard washing the two trucks when Mr. Brodie and his boys drove up. They parked, let the dust settle, and got out.

Tyrell tossed his sponge into a bucket. "Right on time."

Dad turned off the water.

Mr. Brodie had called the night before, but all Dad told Danny and Tyrell was that he and his boys wanted to come over. Billy and Ben had some atoning to do.

Danny and Tyrell had to look that word up. "It means to make things right, or to apologize."

Danny thought, *Too late for that.*

"There's something else," Dad said. "It seems we have Harmon's rifle. You boys know anything about that?"

They told him how they got it and why they kept it.

Dad considered their story, somber. Then he shook his head and turned away. But they both saw the grin he tried to hide.

"Morning, Harmon," Dad said. He nodded to Billy and Ben. "Boys."

Billy and Ben dipped their heads but didn't look at any of them.

Mr. Brodie looked up at the blue high desert sky. "Too nice a morning for something like this, but it's got to be done." He turned to Danny. "First off, Danny, I owe you an apology for going after your dog. You were right all along, and I . . . well . . . I went along believing in a lie."

He turned to Billy and Ben. Looked at them, as if inspecting a flat tire. "They tried to concoct a story about how they lost the rifle. I'm not so old I can't see through a tall one. Now I know that they went out to wander around in the night with the rifle. They made a little campfire and saw your dog."

Mr. Brodie looked at Billy.

"Billy took a shot, just to scare it." He paused, looked down, and quietly added, "I'm glad the dog survived."

Danny felt his honest regret. "Me too, Mr. Brodie," he said, almost in a whisper.

"We've settled with it, Harmon," Dad said. "Banjo's got a new home with good people, and you were kind enough to give Danny the pup. I think we can all just let this go and start again."

"Thank you."

Danny eyed Billy, not feeling generous about letting him off the hook. Not without the whole story coming out.

But Ben looked sorry.

Tyrell stood frowning, arms crossed.

Dad lifted his chin to Danny. "Run in and get Harmon his rifle."

"Yes, sir."

It stood in the back corner of the closet, alongside their grandfather's Winchester. Danny pulled it out and looked up at the two beer bottles on the shelf above the coat rack. He started to reach for them but stopped and stared at them. He pursed his lips and closed the closet door.

Mr. Brodie took the rifle, checked the safety, and tucked it under his arm, barrel down. "The boys have something to say."

Mr. Brodie waited, staring at the dirt around his boots as if too disappointed or embarrassed to look at his own sons.

Dad waited.

Danny and Tyrell waited.

When Billy and Ben failed to speak, Mr. Brodie looked up. Waiting.

Ben shifted from one foot to the other. "Uh . . . we, um . . . we . . ."

He averted his eyes.

Billy glowered at Danny. "Sorry we shot at your dog. Sorry you lost it. Sorry we caused you trouble."

Silence.

Ben found his nerve. "Now we gotta work for you. Dad says ten hours."

More silence.

"Well," Dad said. "Been thinking about that since

Harmon came up with the idea last night. I think I have just the thing for you boys, and it may take all ten of those hours."

Danny looked at Tyrell.

Tyrell shrugged. *Who knows?*

Dad pointed to the pasture. "See that stump out there?"

. . .

Mr. Brodie drove off, leaving Billy and Ben to the stump.

Danny and Tyrell went up to Tyrell's upstairs bedroom, watching out the window, trying to stifle the laughs bursting up in both of them.

"Look . . . I can't believe they don't see him," Tyrell said.

"They will."

Billy and Ben had no idea that Ricky's crazy steer was pawing the dirt, not five feet behind them.

Danny had to wipe tears away to see. "It's coming, it's going to snort."

Ben was the first to turn around, and when he did, people all the way over to Bend could hear his scream.

Billy dropped his pick and staggered backward. When he saw the steer, he leaped clear out of the stump hole.

The second snort sent them sprinting for the fence.

The steer bolted in the opposite direction.

Danny and Tyrell laughed so hard and so loud that Billy and Ben looked toward the house.

"Stop, stop," Danny howled. "They'll hear us."

But they couldn't stop cracking up.

The Brodie boys dug ten hours, but they never did get that stump out.

But Danny and Tyrell did, shouting, "For Banjo!" when the roots finally broke free.

Acknowledgments

Being in the flow of writing a novel is often a thrill. Revision, especially, is a time when my world stops, and I get lost in rethinking and reworking.

And then there are the times when I have to fight myself—procrastination, laziness, distraction, imagination freeze. But I have ways to get back in the saddle, so to speak. And my favorite way back is by seeking out experts and early readers who can give me feedback.

My most sincere appreciation in the writing of *Banjo* goes out to friends who helped me along the way.

Tammy Sutter, for her kindness, endless support, and encouragement; Brian and Brooke Winters, bull rider and barrel racer, for keeping a sharp eye on my ranch and rodeo details; Wendy Lamb, my one-and-only-ever editor, and friend; and Dana Carey, keen-eyed, ultra-dog-loving assistant editor—thank you both for the gift of your exquisite editorial skills; and to my writing friends, Jessica Maxwell, who tells me that I'm better than I think I am, and Brian Geraths, for our many conversations on writing and the art of living well. And finally a huge thank-you to my brilliant young prepublication reviewers: Tye Barron (grade 6), Olive Cochran (grade 5), and Wyatt Sydnor (grade 5).

With gratitude also to these experts: Tom Dorrance, Cherry Hill, Buck Brannaman, Kayla Starnes, Ty Murray, Mark Rashid, Monty Roberts, Joe Camp, Susan Richards, and Clinton Anderson. Thank you.

About the Author

Graham Salisbury grew up in the Hawaiian Islands, where his family has lived since 1820. He graduated from California State University and received an MFA from Vermont College of Fine Arts, where he was a member of the founding faculty of the MFA program in writing for children. He is the author of twenty multiple-award-winning books, including *The Hunt for the Bamboo Rat*, *Under the Blood-Red Sun*, *House of the Red Fish*, *Blue Skin of the Sea*, *Lord of the Deep*, *Night of the Howling Dogs*, *Eyes of the Emperor*, and the Calvin Coconut series for younger readers. He lives in Lake Oswego, Oregon.

grahamsalisbury.com